Acknowledgements

Many thanks go out to friends & family who helped without hesitation; Mark Struckmann for his amazing eye for photography, Ruth Muck for her outstanding editing skills, my gorgeous models, Stephanie Conboy & Tyler Ferington, my parents for helping with research and sitting hours on end listening to me read each chapter, and my dearest husband, Tom, for creating such an incredible book cover.

Dedication

This book is dedicated to my God for His grace & love and showing me that "all things are possible," to my parents for their constant love and encouragement, and to my family, Tom, Tyler, Rebekah, and Madeline, I love you always.

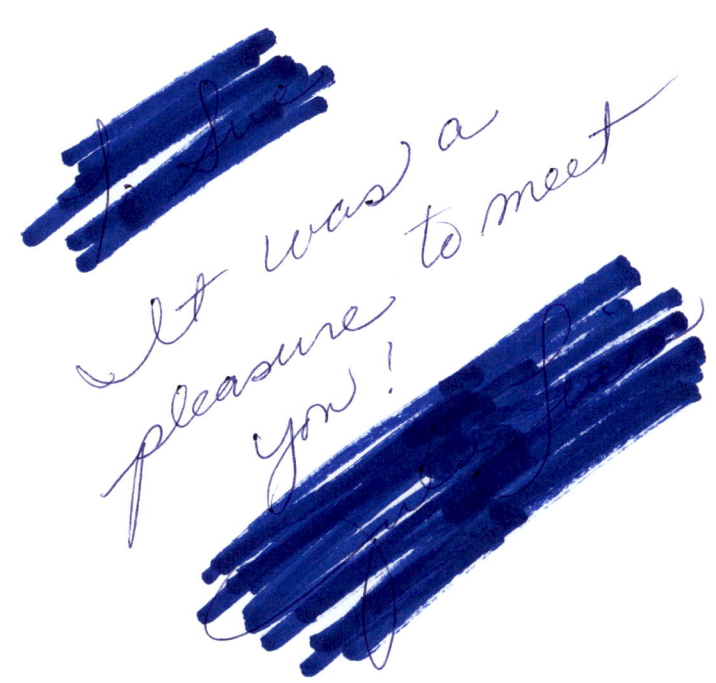

To Sue

It was a pleasure to meet you!

Southern Beauty

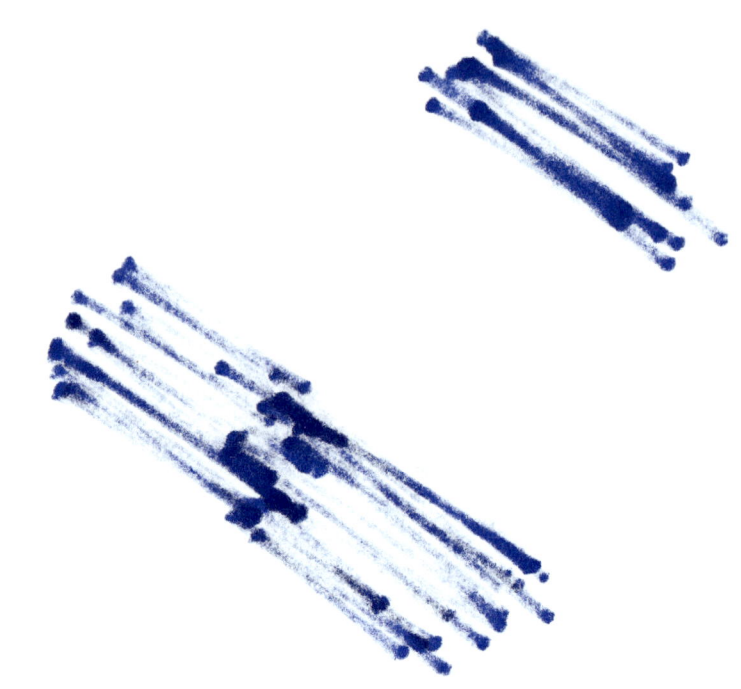

Chapter 1

January 1861

"Pay attention McPherson, we're being summoned," A sharp voice broke Lieutenant David McPherson's daydream of his family who had seemed to be right in front of him.

David had been gazing into the clear waters of the pond that lay next to his regiment's camp. A slim handsome man with broad shoulders stared back at him with a grin. His sandy blonde hair and thick eyebrows hid in the shadows of the pond's waters. He threw a rock to shatter what once was his own reflection. The rock slowly sank into the marsh below. David had received many honors for his heroics since he joined the army. Although he loved the life of a soldier, he was ready to return to his family.

David adjusted his uniform and made his way toward camp. He faintly heard the commander of his unit speaking as he approached.   General George Meade stood in front of his tent and gathered the men around to discuss his plans to prevent further conflicts between the states.

"It is settled then, Lieutenant, you ride out immediately," said Meade. David had been still reminiscing; family gatherings around the fireplace, his mother's delicious shepherd's pie he could almost taste, his sister's lovely singing voice that accompanied him at the piano, and his father's nightly readings of the newest novels that had come from the city. A smile crept upon his face as he imagined the day he would return, "two weeks," he whispered to himself with a sigh.

"From the look of that smile, you must be pleased with my choice," said Meade.

"Sir?" David now realizing the General was talking directly to him.

"Anyone else care to join him on this quest?" asked Meade.

"We will," a heavyset man with a full beard and a tall self-assured man with a mustache came out of the silent crowd of young soldiers. They were friends of David's. Master Sergeant Jacob Evans and Sergeant Preston Myers gladly accepted to once again ride alongside their long time comrade-in-arms.

Jacob was a quiet man with a soft-spoken voice and a kind face. His dark black hair and beard had been turning gray, showing his many years. Jacob was married to Emma and loved her dearly. He only had three more months until his enlistment was up, and he looked forward to meeting his newborn son, Daniel.

Preston, a tall, heavily muscled, confident man intimidated everyone with whom he came in contact. To him, women were on the earth only for men's pleasures.

3

Though the women didn't trust him, neither did the men. People who knew him wondered whose side he would fight. When they would ask him, he simply would say, "My side."

Although, very different men, David loved them both and considered them brothers he never had. Their friendship was made the day their lives intersected in Harrisburg when they each enlisted and were assigned to the same unit. The three were inseparable.

"Men, this is a serious situation. We need that map and if possible, I want his strategic battle plans too," Meade explained to the men. "This mission comes from the highest level; don't disappoint me."

"Yes, sir," said the men in unison.

"A Lieutenant Colonel from Virginia is gaining popularity among the Southern military brass," Meade explained.

Lieutenant Colonel Robert E. Lee's loyalties were wavering due to family obligations in Virginia. This was known even by the newly elected President, Abraham Lincoln, therefore it was vital that before Virginia seceded something had to be done. The plan was to elect General

Meade's elite team to ride to South Carolina undetected by the newly formed Confederate Regulation Army and retrieve strategic military plans including a map of the North and South created by balloonist John Steiner. This was imperative for he had the only accurate map that could lead the Union into the path of victory. The map was given as a gift to Lee and was supposedly on him at all times. He currently resided at one of his family's plantations in Charleston, where he was secretly visiting with the newly appointed General of the Confederate Army. Unbeknownst to Lee, there was a mole reporting his every move since South Carolina seceded in December.

David being the only Lieutenant among the men was elected to lead the mission.

"He is a well respected hero of the Army, and a dear friend of mine whom I met at West Point. Treat him with respect if you need to capture him. Understood?" General Meade explained with sadness in his voice and a frown upon his face.

"Yes sir," answered David with a salute. He silently mouthed the words, "capture him?" to his companions.

The men got upon their saddled horses, grabbing their sabers and revolvers on the way. Under his breath, David cursed the dangerous plan the commander ordered. The three men and their horses galloped off, leaving behind Salisbury, and the many women of Preston's nightly pleasures.

# # #

Beyond the thick dusty clouds, a ray of sunshine peered through and shone upon an immaculate plantation, surrounding it with fields of exquisite flowers that seemed to be an endless array of bouquets. Inside, the rooms were handsomely decorated with a man's touch: a quiet fire burning in the fireplace, before it a sable bear skin rug, and a hat rack that once held a colonel's hat. The cupboards were sufficiently stacked with an extravagant abundance of liquor.

Below in the cellar was wine, fermenting, as it silently waited to be opened. Against the wall hung a new Secession Flag; beside it stood an impeccable, sturdy black musket with a bayonet. Up the flowing oak and marble staircase were elegant bedrooms of crimson velvet. Out on the terrace, a ravishingly beautiful young lady posed in the noon sun, eagerly awaiting her mentor.

Johanna Lee breathed in the deep countryside air. Her long golden hair blew in the timid breeze. Her emerald eyes twinkled in the sun's light. Her ivory skin hid behind an eloquently decorated pink parasol that matched her silken gown of layers of lace that fit tightly from her full breasts to her curving hips and continued outward, covering her from the waist to the marble floor. Johanna Lee had lived here, in her uncle's estate, since her parents fled the country two months ago for Paris. She was left behind for her safety and her reputation. Although it was beautiful, she longed to be near family.

Johanna gripped a letter in her hands. The letter brought her comfort and made her slightly smile through her tears.

It was a letter from her uncle that had been sent to her recently. She reread it;

My Dearest Niece,

I hope this letter finds you in good health. I am sorry I haven't sent for you. It has become difficult for me to travel without suspicion from my superiors. I will be meeting G.T. at Fort Moultrie and unable to retrieve you myself. You will be sent an escort instead to take you to Arlington. I will try to meet you at the inn where the Otter resides before your departure. I have made arrangements for all servants to work for John Grady's plantation. He is a good man, he will provide housing, and pay them handsomely for their service. They will leave within the week. Please take with you my favorite weekly reading material that was given to me by a dear friend who likes ballooning. What ever the cost you must keep it hidden. Trust no one. If for some reason I cannot meet you, please retrieve my box of cigars. It will be at the cottage near your father's preferred drink. You know of which I speak. Our lives may very well depend on it. Therefore it is imperative that you follow my instructions with the utmost discretion. I am sorry to put you at risk, but I know that I can depend and trust in you. Keep safe. May God bless your travels!

With Love,

R.E. Lee

Johanna thought about each sentence. She knew although her uncle had been at the Custiss-Lee Mansion in Arlington after leaving his post in Texas, he hadn't been able to retrieve her due to the rising conflict between the states. Now that South Carolina had seceded and Virginia silently spoke of following, it was harder for him to travel without causing controversy.

# # #

The sun's light disappeared along with its warmth, leaving only a chilling breeze that made the stench of the horses' sweat inflame the men's nostrils. A whistle sang through the forest's trees and the dusty trail the men were following became harder to see the further they traveled. Only a small clearing before them shone of the moon's light. Throughout the woods an array of twinkling lights made the blackened woods seem enchanted.

"It's awfully cold out for fireflies," Preston noticed the lights.

"I don't think those are fireflies. You are just noticing animals watching us from the woods, their eyes are reflecting the moonlight," explained Jacob. "Some people think these woods are enchanted."

"Wow. That's amazing. There must be a hundred of them in there," said Preston.

"Enchanted? Do tell," David asked. "This trip is going to take long enough. We need something to keep us awake."

"That's right, Jacob, you are always good for a story, especially when you had a few too many," Preston chimed in and David laughed.

"If it will get you guys to quit complaining about our mission, I will." Jacob laughed too.

Jacob began to tell mystical tales of fairies that supposedly live among the leaves. Preston and David listened with much anticipation as if they were small children listening to their grandfather pass on generations of tales.

# # #

Lieutenant Colonel Robert E. Lee, who had recently arrived from Virginia, was meeting privately with Charleston's newest Confederate General Brigadier P.G.T. Beauregard at Fort Moultrie just south of the plantation where Johanna lived. Lee found it to be a gift that had fallen into his lap when she was left in his care right before South Carolina seceded in December. He would be able to use Johanna's unfortunate circumstance to his advantage. Therefore he decided to wait for the opportune moment to retrieve her. The moment had finally arrived.

Lee folded a letter and motioned Private Malcolm Graystone over. The handsome Private walked over with a tinge of pride shown in his steps.

"Yes sir?" he asked with a grin and a salute.

"At ease Private," Lee grinned back with a wink and a salute. Though Malcolm was one of his men from the 2nd Calvary regiment, he also was his aide, whom he had grown fond of over the last three months. Lee looked forward to introducing him to his niece. "I want you to personally retrieve Miss Lee and escort her to the Custiss-Lee Mansion where my wife, Mary, will be waiting for her. My plans have changed and I will be staying a little longer to meet with General Beauregard, so I will not be able to take her myself." His smile widened and Graystone knew he had a little more planned than a trip for him and Johanna.

"I will ride out immediately, sir," smiled Malcolm.

"Thanks private. I am hoping to meet you and Miss Lee at our cottage before you leave. Miss Lee has something in her possession that I must have before you go. I have sent someone ahead to quietly bring in supplies and leave just as quietly. If for some reason our plans are interrupted, go straight there immediately. Here is a map I made for you to get there," Lee handed Malcolm the map. "Johanna knows the way. I have sent her a letter informing her of our plans."

"Yes, sir," said Malcolm with a determined look on his face. "I won't let you down. I will do whatever it takes to keep her safe," Malcolm assured him.

"That is why I am sending you," said Lee, "I know that I can trust you, especially with my niece."

Chapter 2

"Miss Patricia. Why you look lovely in your red bonnet! What brings you here today?" Johanna asked.

"Hello Johanna. I came by to see if you were coming for tea this afternoon?" Patricia asked.

"Oh, I'm feeling a bit tired, I think I need to rest, perhaps another day. Please tell the ladies I said hello, will you?" Johanna forced a smile, hoping Patricia would just leave without asking questions.

"Of course I will." Patricia said while her eyes searched the foyer and the rooms that adjoined.

"Goodbye then," Johanna said as she began closing the door.

Patricia put her foot in the doorway to prevent the door from closing on her, "A lady should never answer her own door. Where are all the servants?"

"They were giving me a headache," Johanna answered.

"All of them?" questioned Patricia.

Johanna sighed, "If you must know, some were sent to another plantation and I assume others fled. I will be leaving soon anyway my uncle is sending a soldier to escort me to Arlington today."

"Oh dear, we must have you over for dinner before you leave," Patricia said.

"Oh, that is not necessary, really. I have already said my goodbyes," said Johanna.

"Very well then," She gave up. Patricia thought how terribly sad it was that just a few months ago when Johanna's parents fled she had become so secluded. "Maybe

14

you won't leave before the ball on Saturday hosted by the Beauregard's. I heard it's in honor of the cadets firing on the Union ship. All those handsome young cadets from Citadel will be there!"

"Oh then, why I wouldn't miss it for the world." Johanna mimicked Patricia's thick accent with ease and rolled her eyes in disgust. And then she watched Patricia stroll pass the iron-gate, nod to her driver, and step into her carriage.

As Johanna closed the door, her condescending smile disappeared. As she thought about Clarice's party, she felt nauseous. She walked over to the mirror that hung on the wall. She leaned in to get a better look at herself, tears began to swell up in her eyes and she watched them trickle down her rosy cheeks.

It didn't matter that Johanna was alone, she was used to it. Johanna became a recluse since her parents' financial ruin and their embarrassing escape. She preferred to stay home and read. It was a favorite pastime of her mother's and she in turn enjoyed it herself. Since her best friend Abigail wed in September to a lawyer from Georgia and moved to be near his family, she had few friends. She had no one really to be confidantes with except her matchmaking friend Mary Alice, who always tried to set her up to meet the most boorish of snooty men at parties they were expected to attend. The men rarely fussed over her, which didn't bother Johanna in the slightest. She actually welcomed becoming another tapestry on the ballroom walls. She did hate that when the General's daughter, Clarice, came around, Johanna was but forgotten.

Clarice Beauregard was an auburn-haired Cajun-goddess. She was extremely admired by young eligible men for her beautiful looks and her flirtatious nature. Actually the whole family was extremely handsome. Clarice's twin brother, Rene, was one of the most eligible bachelors of the South. During teatime at Miss Patricia's there was so much gossip about Clarice and Rene, Johanna stopped attending them. She only wanted to stay as far away from the women who gossiped, and the men who they gossiped about.

Johanna's heart ached for a new life in Virginia. She longed for the day she would unite with her family. Johanna's tears began to flow even harder now, and she ran up to her room and fell hard onto her bed. At her beside she cradled the last book her parents had given her, an 1859 copy of Blackwood's Magazine, all the way from London. She had it book marked to her favorite novel, by a Miss Austen. She liked it not for the romance, but the family's closeness, especially that of sisters. It was something she had always longed for.

Romance was the last thing on Johanna's mind. She hadn't had much luck with it in the past and she hated the drama that always seemed to accompany it. She had more important things to think on.

Since December, Charleston had become independent from the Union and while many celebrated others were fleeing in fear of Lincoln's army. This fear ran rapidly through Johanna's plantation. Many of the workers fled and the ones who stayed behind began to migrate to their new appointed employer a mile away. Although being in the South slavery was legal, the Lees did not believe in it. Therefore all men who worked were paid in some kind of form. Johanna had many acquaintances who believed differently. She believed no one should be someone's property. They were all handmade by God and should be treated alike. There were several who felt like the Lees but would not fight against it. Johanna just wanted to be away from all the turmoil and the extreme emotions that this controversy stirred up. Virginia seemed like a safer place being near family and those who shared her point of view.

# # #

Private Malcolm Graystone eyed his new dress clothes. His commander had him wear a new Southerner's uniform to ward off any trouble retrieving Johanna. It seemed they just washed a union uniform many times with lye to turn it gray. He laughed at his predicament. Pretending to be someone he wasn't was not new territory for Malcolm. Ahead he spied a local tavern. His stomach growled and he decided to stop for something to eat. Only five miles down the road from his destination was Johanna Lee and if he wasn't so tired and hungry he would have continued on, but his hunger pains began to make him feel weak. He just needed to regenerate, and he would be on his way.

Malcolm couldn't wait to meet the woman his commander told him so much about. He was 21 and ready to start a family. The barmaid approached him and asked him his order. Malcolm decided to order a drink to calm his nerves.

Malcolm didn't realize how much rum he had until he stood up to walk out towards his horse. His head began to spin. He squinted as he scanned the town and noticed a small inn across the road. He decided that it would be best if he met Johanna in the morning. He felt so good that he began to whistle as he staggered toward the inn. He was interrupted by a sweet voice from behind.

"Hello handsome, are you a soldier here to protect little ole me?" the lady asked.

Malcolm turned to see a beautiful sultry woman in a pastel green dress, lace from head to toe, and his heart began to pound. He smirked as his eyes traced her perfect body. He could see the outline of her full breasts through her dress and was immediately smitten.

"Why, ma'm, you're going to need someone to protect you from me," he smiled. The woman blushed as her hungry eyes inspected the handsome soldier.

"Are you going to stay the night there?" she motioned in the direction he was heading. "You must not be from around here. Why don't you come with me, I know where you can find more comfortable accommodations."

"No thank you, Miss." Malcolm declined.

"Well, no self respecting gentleman should stay there, my family owns the mansion on the next street over. Let me escort you there."

He leaned over and kissed her hand, and grinned. "No thank you. I must leave early in the morning. I have a mission to accomplish. Now what is a beautiful lady like you doing here without an escort?"

"Oh, I am shopping for a new bonnet. There are so many now that we receive shipments from London. I always get the newest in fashion. It's a way for me to feel pretty and of course to be the envy of all my dear friends," she giggled.

"Well, I am sure even without the new bonnet you are

envied,' he said.

She smiled a strange shy yet seductive smile at him. "Are you flirting with me?"

"Of course not, just observing," his head seemed in a cloud. He thought to himself that he definitely shouldn't have had that last drink. He had no idea where this was heading and wasn't sure if he should find out. "I've never met a lady like you before."

"And you never will." She said with her seductive smile and slipped her hand into his as they made there way toward the inn. It was now dark, but the inn lit up before them, a welcoming sight especially for Malcolm whose thoughts were getting fuzzier by the minute.

"Thank you ma'am," Malcolm was going to kiss her cheek, but she pressed her body to his and kissed him gently on the mouth.

His lips tasted of alcohol, but they were warm, and her skin tingled as they made their way towards her bare shoulders.

Chapter 3

Early in the morning, the fatigued David, Preston, and Jacob came to an opening in the woods. There lay a vast plantation and a Confederate's home. Jacob and Preston, who fought over the harmonica and the chewing tobacco throughout their trip, were speechless now. Fascinated by the scenery, they deeply inhaled the exhilarating country's fresh air. David, confused at the sight, motioned the men to halt.

"What's the problem McPherson?" asked Jacob.

"There's no one here. It's desolate. No slaves, no soldiers, it's not right," he replied in a hushed tone.

"Do you think it's a trap? Do they know we're coming?" Preston asked with concern.

"Well, if it's a trap, we're going to be the mice. Let's go get our cheese." David said digging his heels into his horse. Preston and Jacob followed behind.

The men vigorously bolted through the front gate.

"Let's split up," David ordered.

Each of the men entered from opposite sides of the house. Jacob opened the servants' entrance door in the back of the mansion. He stepped into the kitchen and found stairs to the cellar and headed down. Preston stepped through the front door with David and made his way toward the stairs to investigate the second floor, while David continued his search on the main floor.

Suddenly, a woman's scream echoed through the halls. David darted upstairs from where the shriek of terror had come. He grasped the oak railing with clenched fingers to pull himself up the stairs faster.

"Keep your dirty Yankee hands off of me!" Johanna

cried recognizing the uniform as she fought to loosen Preston's tight grip. A glimpse of a handsome figure standing in the room's doorway made her tremble, not with fear, more of delight that made her tender skin tingle. Preston's strong hold began to suffocate her; she gasped for air.

"Sure looks like you have your hands full, Preston," David grinned as he began to approach the defenseless Johanna. Pulling her away from Preston, he drew her close to him, pressing her flawless texture next to his. Her emerald eyes gleamed at him and filled his insides with a strong burning flame that ignited as he took a deep breath. His mind helplessly searched for a sense of reality. He could smell her sweet perfumed skin. He felt a desire to taste her red lips upon his own.

"Where's Lieutenant Colonel Lee?" Jacob interrupted. "I've searched the whole premises, he's not here, but I did find this nice aged wine in the cellar. Anyone care to share it with me?" Jacob asked as he held up the wine bottle.

McPherson looked back down at Johanna and pushed

her away from him, keeping a tight grip around her arm. Furious with himself for desiring Johanna, he stepped back away from her and stared her down.

"Where's the Lieutenant Colonel, Miss?" Preston asked her as he undressed her with his provocative eyes.

Johanna stood her ground, "Well, let me think, he could be milking our cow, having tea at Miss Patricia's, or he might be at Fort Moultrie planning to kick your a…"

"That will be enough," David interrupted her. Johanna smiled sarcastically.

"What's your name, beauty?" McPherson asked as she once again stood next to him.

"And wouldn't you like to know?" Johanna boldly asked, surprised by her lack of fear. She made her way to the door.

David grabbed her arm, pulling her fragile body once again to his muscular one. "Yes, I would," he said in a soothing monotone that made her whole body quiver.

Johanna couldn't shake the force he had over her. Her heart pounding against his chest made her feel weak. As she pressed her lips together, she slowly broke the silence that awaited her words. "It's Johanna, Johanna Lee."

"What is this?" Preston asked as he scanned a letter that had been sitting on her dresser.

"That is mine, give it to me!" Johanna insisted, horrified that she could be so foolish to leave her uncle's letter sitting out since she had packed her things earlier, including secretly hiding Lee's map.

"She's got the map! Where is it?" Preston asked with authority. Johanna was silent. David grabbed the letter to read it himself.

"Do you have the plans, the map?" David questioned her.

"I don't know what he was talking about, I couldn't find anything," Johanna lied.

"She's lying," Jacob chimed in.

"Well, let's see," Preston grabbed her belongings she stuffed in a trunk that sat on floor next to the bed. He pulled out clothes, a photograph of her parents, the Blackwood's Magazine and a Harper's Weekly. "You read this rubbish?" He held up the Blackwood's Magazine.

"Where is this inn?" David asked her.

"I will never tell you," Johanna stared at David. She knew that her uncle was talking about the cottage her uncle and father came upon when they were playing hide and seek when they were children.

It was a special place for the Lees. Her parents and she would go there on retreat to get away from the daily life of the high society stresses that came from being a Lee. She remembered just sitting by the fireplace and reading to her parents. Johanna and her uncle dubbed it Otter's Cottage because Johanna had been reading a book on otters and became so fascinated with them she asked her uncle if she could have one for a pet. She remembered him laughing at her question. The cottage was a desolate location by the river. A perfect place she thought, no one even knows it exists. Not until now.

"I think we should search this entire place until we find the map," Jacob said.

"We don't have time. Jacob, do a thorough search of this place. Report back here in five minutes," David ordered with out taking his eyes off of Johanna.

"Look at these," Preston whistled as he held up

Johanna's undergarments. David watched Johanna's face turn red.

Johanna grabbed her clothes out of Preston's hands, "You are a foul creature, a protégé of the Union no doubt." She made David smile. Something he hadn't done in a long while.

Jacob returned, "I couldn't find anything. She had to have taken it already. Did you search her?"

"I will do that," Preston licked his lips as he neared her.

"That is not necessary," David halted Preston with his arm. "We'll just have to take this Southern beauty with us instead." Frustrated for blurting out such a thing he shoved her on the bed.

"Over my dead body!" Johanna exclaimed as she tightened her fists, to pull herself up off the bed.

"That's okay with me," David teased her with a half smile forming on his tanned face, pushing her back down. Slowly she pulled her long golden curls out of her face so she could see once more the vile men who stood above her. She tightly gripped the ends of her vivid yellow dress that matched her hair preventing it from lifting up.

David pulled out his revolver and pointed it at Johanna. Everyone in the room stood in shock by David's harsh actions.

"Okay, Miss Johanna Lee, pack your things, you're coming with us," said David.

"What? This is mad! What will we gain by taking her?" Jacob questioned David's sanity.

"If she wants to live she will show us how to get to this inn," David looked at his men. "As soon as we get what we came for, we will release her, but for now she is detrimental to our mission."

"Are you sure you know what you are doing?" asked Jacob in a whisper.

Preston laughed at David's irrational behavior in making his brazen decision, "now he is thinking like a soldier."

David eyed both men without answering Jacob. He was unsure if he had made the right decision but refused to acknowledge it. He had just set their course in motion and wasn't about to turn back now.

David stared down Johanna who now looked frightened. "Miss, you are now a prisoner of the U.S. Army."

Chapter 4

Private Malcolm Graystone was eating breakfast in the common room of the inn he stayed the night before. Waking up he couldn't remember when he last said goodbye to the beautiful woman from the night before. He looked around his room and was pleased he didn't see any signs of her presence. Thankful he was smart enough to end the tête-à-tête with the captivating woman before it even began. He had no idea of her name and was glad he would not have to explain his intentions after their steamy kiss. Although it would not help him in winning Johanna over, her kiss seemed to be entrenched in his mind. He still was glad, he didn't need any more complications than he had already encountered.

Malcolm walked out to his horse, petting him as he watched the morning sun rise. He was ready to take Johanna to Arlington, and if everything went according to plan, he would court her, and maybe eventually take her hand in marriage. This would make his life much easier, getting closer to his ultimate goal, personally and financially. He needed a break and making her happy and his commander ever so proud, would change things for him. Taking the reigns on the horse, he lifted himself up, and began to ride.

# # #

While Johanna grabbed her trunk and repacked the things that Preston had taken out Jacob took David aside.

"What about the map?" Jacob whispered.

"I know she has it. Before this trip is over, we will have everything we have come for," David answered.

"What do you think is in these papers that are so important?" asked Jacob.

"I believe they are military strategies and maps planned out by Lee himself," said David.

"I thought that was just a story, the plans I mean," said Jacob.

"No, he made them. It's just whoever gets to them first. If the Confederates get their hands on it, we will lose more than Fort Sumter," said David.

Johanna silently went along with them, knowing there was no one around even if she did scream. She wasn't worried about her uncle's map that she strategically placed in her mother's locket she wore hidden around her neck, but if they found it, they would capture him for his betrayal to the Union. She had to keep it hidden, but when the soldier pulled out his weapon on her she was frightened, and she decided to lead them to Otter's Cottage even if it meant her uncle would be in danger.

She needed time to think. Maybe she would delay

their trip and give her uncle time to flee and then wait for the opportunity to escape, or if she was sly enough, she could learn what they were planning and notify the Confederate Army as soon as they released her. Either way her life was now in danger and she was on the edge of a cliff she wasn't sure she was going to have to jump or be pushed off.

# # #

A day of difficult riding made Johanna exhausted and her insides ache. Her fingers were linked together around David's waist. He hadn't spoken to her or shown any kind of compassion towards her since the first time they met. When he did speak to her, he only spoke in short words that were cold and unsympathetic. Though she knew she was in danger and so was her uncle, her curiosity increased as they rode. David intrigued her and this won out over her feelings of fear. She knew they had felt some kind of connection the first time they met. Her impetuous thoughts burned within her. She then tightened the grip she had on him, bringing his muscular back toward the warmth of her body.

"Let go, you're holding on too tight." David coughed.

Johanna had been the only thing on his mind since he first laid eyes on her. Her gentle touch made his heart flutter like a school kid in his first crush. Passion interfered with his normal thought process. David was angry with himself, for he had no time for romance and no interest in marriage. Since Johanna had been around, he seemed to have forgotten what his general mission was.

"It's Johanna's fault for being so beautiful and smelling so-damn her," he whispered to himself, he was furious with her for being so irresistibly lovely. He had no idea why he had not listened to Jacob who tried to convince him not to take the naïve Johanna. But, as soon as they retrieved the letter from her he knew she had to show them how to get to her family's cottage. It sounded absurd at first, but it was the only way to complete their mission and besides no harm would come to her. They needed the Lieutenant Colonel's papers and they would do anything to get them, the map and his military plans.

Thoughts of her sweet love clouded his mind. She held him more tightly as if she could read it.

"She must stay away," David whispered under his steamy breath, so only he could hear.

"Did you say something," Johanna questioned his murmur.

Her voice was that of an angel's. "You can ride with Preston tomorrow I don't need a Southern whore riding with me," David brutally forced himself to say as he bit his tender lip, waiting for her reaction to his chilling accusation.

Stunned by his harsh words, she remained silent, which was very difficult for her. She let go of the tight hold she had on him and then turned her head away in frustration and shame. Although her eyes were filled with tears, she refused to let him affect her again.

Johanna had shown the men the way to her family's special place, and it hurt her to share it with anyone other than her parents and her uncle. She had pointed out to Jacob that it was beyond the trees near the river. Preston went ahead to scout it out. He returned with a look of distress.

"The cottage is ahead, it's completely deserted, but oddly enough, it's fully stocked with food and supplies. I think someone was here, but left in a hurry," said Preston.

"We can stay there for the night until we decide what to do," David insisted. "We will keep our eyes open for any visitors."

David looked behind him to see the confused look on Johanna's face. Then he stopped the horse in front of the cottage and jumped off, taking the hand of Johanna to help her down.

Johanna couldn't keep her eyes off the little house that had fallen into disrepair. She hadn't been here in over a decade. She felt a flicker of sadness as she thought about being with her family here enjoying the simple life they never had time for, and no longer could enjoy. Her thoughts switched back to the ghastly man before her who was trying to take her hand and help her down off the horse.

Taking his hand briefly, they both felt a bolt of lightning strike their unsuspecting hearts, although their reactions differed. David held his breath surprised by the strong connection he felt when they touched hands. Johanna too angry, ignored the shock, and stepped down. She came face to face with him and with a blunt slap, she reddened his unshaven face.

"I am sure you are quite familiar with ladies of the evening, being in the military and all. Here in the South we are much more than ladies. Just because the women in the North are easy, never mistake me for one of your harlots again. I am above you in manners and in class and you, my sir, will never have the fortune to love a lady like me, in body and in heart."

David was taken back by her slap and her harsh words toward him. He knew he deserved it, but still felt the shock of being scolded. He realized he was still holding her other hand. Her words were sharp as a knife, but her hand was so soft it pierced his heart and as she let go, her touch lingered.

"I'm going to wash," she looked the men up and down. "I am sure you men are accustomed to smelling like that, but I am not." She marched towards the river ever so proud of her last words to the man she had learned to despise.

The men all stood staring at one another, and then Preston smelled his armpits and shrugged his shoulders. They all looked back at Johanna who was walking toward the river's edge.

Preston laughed at his friend's encounter, while he tied the horses up to the nearest tree.

"She's got fire in her blood, that one,"

"Shut up and go make dinner," David glared, trying to hide his pride that had been damaged far worse than his cheek. He rubbed his face and stared in Johanna's direction.

"What do we do now, McPherson?" Jacob interrupted.

"We need to stay out of sight and keep watch. There is no way Lee would leave his own niece stranded. He'll come or he'll send someone for her," said David.

Down at the river's edge, Johanna was enjoying the refreshing waters. She felt so calm and serene as she washed her face of dirt and grime. The currents tickled her velvet skin as she washed her hands and arms. She inhaled the pleasant odor of the forest's evergreens. Losing herself in the congenial surroundings, she reminisced of her uncle and her playing hide-and-seek in the woods when she was young. Although she was concerned for his safety, a smile formed on her thin lips, she closed her eyes. She hadn't come here since she was very young and she couldn't bear the thought of remembering each wonderful memory. But, now she felt oddly comforted.

Johanna looked around making sure no one was watching her while she undressed. Although her petticoat would not leave her body, she wanted to wash her dirty dress. She leaned in closer for a better advantage point when she plunged right into the ice cold water. The river was unexpectedly colder than she thought and screamed from the shock. She began to panic when she realized she had fallen out of reach of the river's edge, Johanna did not know how to swim. She screamed for help as she gasped for air. Her heart beat madly in her chest as if it was about to burst. She opened her mouth to scream again, but only inhaled the water. Her hands desperately searched for something to keep her afloat, her petticoat clung to her and her helpless body weakened as she struggled to stay alive. She heard a voice from the water's bank and thought she could see David peering down at her, a panicked look on his face.

Diving into the water, David grabbed Johanna by the hair, standing her up on her feet. Out of fear she did not realize she had only been in three feet of water. She fell again and he drove her close to him and picked her fragile body up in his muscular arms. As David pulled her limp form onto the rocky shore, he held her tight, fearing if he let go, she would die. He caressed her colorless face.

He whispered into her ear, "Don't die on me, not now, not when you just came into my life, I need you here with me. Please don't die my precious Southern Beauty." Surprised at his own words, he gently kissed her dampened cheek.

Johanna began to cough, her eyes slowly opened to the handsome face of David looking down at her. He watched her pale gray eyes return to their emerald color and her purple lips turn back into velvet. He could feel her heart pound against his chest.

Johanna's fiery breath became heavier, her whole frail body belonging to David. Only minutes passed but it felt like hours, her insides burned with volcanic pleasures that exploded each time she inhaled. A passion they never felt before, her untouched ivory skin invited his touch. David's gaze was fixed onto her velvet lips and he slowly bent down to taste them. Johanna could feel his steamy breath colliding toward her own. Inches away from her lips, she brought the passionate moment to a complete halt.

"Get off me you, brute!" she said coldly as her fists began to beat his chest with what strength she had left. David's sapphire eyes questioned her hardened look. He wondered how such passion could turn to such rage. Was he mistaken about her feelings, their connection? Was he so sure of himself?

"What's wrong Beauty? Am I too much for you?" he teased with his boyish grin.

Quickly the fogginess in her head cleared, she remembered his whispers when he thought she had drowned. Maybe she just imagined it, but his words began to affect her. She eyed him with curiosity. David had a hold of her wrists to prevent her from attack when her fists froze. It was silent once again, she watched David lean over her,

Johanna closed her eyes giving into the yearning she suddenly had for his kiss. She pulled her chin up waiting for his lips to meet hers.

David smirked trying not to laugh out loud. He bent over closer as she opened her eyes to meet his once again, and David grabbed her dress, that sat in a pile next to her, and threw them upon her undressed body.

"Hurry, dinner's waiting," David said turning toward the old wooden cottage. Horrified, Johanna's face turned ghostly white before it could redden, and she fell unconscious, hiding her humiliation.

David could hardly bear to turn to her once more, but when she didn't make a sound behind him, he saw her lifeless body lay upon the rocks.

Chapter 5

*D*avid wrapped Johanna's dress around her, picked her up in his arms and brought her to the cottage.

"What's wrong with her?" Preston inquired with a look of confusion that matched Jacob's.

"She passed out. Could you guys go get some wood for the fire?" David asked without looking at them.

Following orders both men abruptly left the cabin. David laid her on the abandoned bed. He gently stroked her long dampened hair. Trying to coax her awake, he whispered softly in her ear, "Miss Lee, can you hear me?"

Her swollen eyes opened enough to see David's golden face. She felt worse than she had ever felt; she was hungry, weak, and humiliated.

"You're going to be all right my Southern Beauty," he continued to whisper, "I will never let anything happen to you." Johanna heard him but she was powerless to sleep and she again belonged to the void of darkness.

That night, Johanna awoke to see the cheery face of Preston as he held tight her hand. Alcohol reeked on his breath and before she could speak, his coarse lips came down hard upon hers.

"Get away from her, Myers!" David fiercely called out as he gripped Preston's hair tightly between his clenched fingers, pulling him away from the frightful Johanna.

"Sorry about that, he had a little too much whiskey. He won't bother you again," David reassured the frightened Johanna. She fell back into her deepened slumber, forgetting about Preston's advances. She only dreamt of what she felt in her heart, a love for the man who sat by her bed, jealous stricken of Preston's affection toward her. His hidden rage kept secret with his flaming desire for her.

Throughout the day, David would barely talk to her let alone look at her. She was surprised how easily it was to befriend Jacob. He seemed more like a friendly butcher than a soldier. They talked of books and of family. With an occasional added word from David like, "hmmm." Preston spent most of the day outdoors scouting and gathering firewood, which suited Johanna just fine. She felt very uncomfortable when he was around. He would stare at her with eagerness as he lurked in the dark corner of the room. He seemed almost like a black cat ready to pounce on its prey. She tried not to notice him staring at her when he thought no one was looking. His sinister manner only intensified when she found him hovering over her while she slept.

David tried to keep Preston's advances at bay, especially when he had found him smelling her hair. Without warning David lunged at him and threw Preston against the wall. Preston, who was caught off guard, had suddenly felt the sting of the wall on his back with a powerful force that sent him straight to the wooden floor.

"Keep your hands off of her!" David warned in a protective tone.

"Oh, I see you are saving her for yourself?" Preston questioned David and laughed as he rubbed his cheek and picked himself up.

"Just knock it off or I will report your insubordination to our commander," threatened David.

"Come on McPherson I was just having a little fun," Preston tried to laugh it off.

"Keep in mind we have a mission. Let's stick to it. We are not here to have fun," ordered David.

As Preston walked out of the cabin to retreat from the situation, he leaned into Johanna and whispered," You won't always have McPherson to protect you."

"Protect me from what, pray tell." Johanna boldly stood her ground unaffected by his warning.

Preston did not answer her question, turned and exited.

After David protected her Johanna noticed him in a different light. Throughout the day his manner became more relaxed and he almost seemed friendly. She watched him as he bantered with Jacob to everyone's amusement. She even once found herself laughing out loud and had to cover her mouth to be discrete.

That evening, David read a few lines out of her magazine as they all sat by the fireplace.

"Is this collection about romance?" David asked her.

Embarrassed Johanna covered, "It's more about family," she took it out of his hand "I think that is enough for today thank you."

"Those are Miss Austen's writings?" Jacob asked.

"Yes," said Johanna.

"Oh Emma loves her stories. They are all about romance and love. It's a girl thing David," Jacob said.

"Now I am curious," David asked Johanna scratching his unshaven chin. "How much do you know about it?"

"Know about what?" Johanna asked confused.

"Know about romance and love?" David smiled teasing her.

Johanna refused to answer his question and put her magazine away. Jacob grinned at David's question while

David smirked at her uncomfortable reaction.

Afterward David taught Johanna a card game in which she played quite well. She promised to teach him backgammon some day, and quickly retracted in embarrassment of the situation.

"I guess I forgot for a second where I was," she said. They all laughed.

During the two days she was held captive, they secretly watched one another when they thought neither was looking. It didn't go unnoticed by Jacob. He began to feel fondly toward Johanna and actually felt obliged to remind David that there was no way it would ever work out between them.

"What are you talking about Jacob? I feel nothing for her," said David.

"McPherson, just remember what you are here for. Besides, could you imagine..." Jacob said.

"No, I cannot, and I would not," interrupted David.

"Just don't get involved in something you are never intending to finish. I have spent time talking to her, she reminds me of my own niece. She doesn't deserve your false advances," said Jacob.

"I have no intentions of any kind, she is a Southerner, Lee's niece, and a royal pain," proclaimed David.

"Are you falling for her?" questioned Jacob with a look of concern on his face.

"Are you insane? Are you listening to anything I am telling you?" David asked in denial. "If she needs a companion, Preston can have her."

Jacob eyed David not believing him, "If you haven't fallen in love with her, leave her be, it will only end in heartache for the both of you!"

"Fallen in love with her?" David repeated. "That's absurd! You seem to be the only one enticed by her beauty. I am about done with this, this mission and this conversation."

# # #

In the dusk of the early morning amidst their slumber, Johanna awoke and scanned the room. She saw

Jacob and Preston asleep across the room slightly snoring. She quickly sat up and thought in a brief instant she should try to escape. The idea was quickly extinguished when she realized David lay on the floor beside her fast asleep. She tried to get a better look at him, so she leaned over a bit too much and then she fell right on top of him. Johanna could feel his fiery breath upon hers though he did not make a sound. Her body froze, though it was inflamed with fireworks that exploded a thousand times inside her. She wanted more. She longed for his touch. Did he have any idea she had fallen upon him? Or fallen for him?

David had been afraid to fall asleep since the last episode with Preston. He stayed by Johanna like a watchdog. He couldn't sleep anyway. He had been going over in his mind what he whispered to her at the river. He was appalled that he felt that way toward someone so difficult and proud. Her attitude toward them insinuated that they were beneath her. He didn't know why he wanted her. What she needed was to be put in her place. He eyed her in the dark when he noticed movement above him. When she leaned over to get a closer look at him he saw her falling and immediately braced himself for the impact. He was going to scold her back into her bed, but something happened when their bodies touched. Johanna's warmth enveloped him. His very soul steamed with fire. He wanted to wrap his arms around her, embrace her, and love her. He couldn't open his eyes it was too much.

Johanna, inches away from his tempting lips, slowly came down to touch them gently with her own. Breath to breath, lips barely touching, Johanna hoped for some tender response to her closeness. David began to snore.

"You Yankee fool," Johanna whispered as she picked herself up off of him and made her way back into bed.

David covered his laugh with a cough. He turned over so she could not see his face. Again without knowing it, she made him laugh. What made him do such a thing? David pondered this until the sun rose. Holding the lovely Johanna in his arms was the only thing he could think of since they met. Was it his devotion to his mission? No, the mission could not be further from his thoughts. It's only Johanna that he wants or ever wants. She was right he was a fool. They both stared into the night waiting for the morning to arrive thinking only of each other and the missed opportunity of passion.

# # #

To Johanna's relief, morning finally came.

"Where are you going?" Johanna whispered to Jacob as he started toward the door.

"Well, good morning Miss Lee," surprised to see her awake he asked, "Did you sleep well?"

"I guess, the best I can under the circumstances," she shrugged with a half smile.

"I am going to get wood, would you like to join me for a walk?" He asked cheerfully as he held the door open for her.

Tiptoeing past David, she shook her head in disappointment. She followed Jacob out the door and they both disappeared into the woods.

"Are you married, Mr. Evans?" Johanna asked.

"Yes, my wife is in Harrisburg waiting for my

return," he answered not noticing the set of footprints that lay on the muddy ground next to their own.

"Is that where we are going?" Johanna asked.

"No. We are headed to New Orleans. We need to get out of enemy territory," he answered.

"Isn't Louisiana on its way to succession too?" she asked.

"It isn't yet. We have a contact there. We must be meeting them soon," Jacob looked at Johanna who seemed confused. "I am not sure what David has planned for you. Don't worry though, I know him, and he would never jeopardize your safety and I will make sure of it." He smiled and looked down at her in a fatherly sort of way.

"Oh, you don't need to worry about me. I can take care of myself," she insisted.

"Yes, I could confirm that," he said and they both smiled.

"Are we waiting for my uncle?" she asked.

"I am not sure what we're doing to tell the truth. This is McPherson's show," explained Jacob.

"Oh, he can sometimes be so difficult. Is that a

Northern thing or does he not have a mother to teach him manners, especially around ladies?" asked Johanna.

"Ah, he's not so bad once you get to know him. He has a great Christian family actually. And to tell you the truth they would be appalled he is treating you so unkindly. I am hesitant to go on any further, Miss Lee," he paused for her attention, "he is like a brother to me."

"I'm sorry. I spoke out of place," she agreed.

Jacob smiled at her, "I've never seen him act this way before and we have been friends for a very long time."

"Whatever do you mean?" Johanna asked with much interest.

Jacob didn't want to say anymore for he knew David felt more than he was letting on. "He is generally the perfect gentleman, ladies love him, men respect him, and well, ever since we met you, he has been, let's just say different."

"I see," Johanna didn't know what to make of this.

"Don't take him too seriously. He likes to antagonize you," Jacob said in a whisper.

"I got that," she said. "I think he needs someone to teach him a good lesson."

"Would that be you?" he asked in a laugh.

"Is he married?" asked Johanna ignoring Jacob's questioned.

"Not yet, but his mother is trying to marry him off," Jacob explained.

"Marry him off?" Johanna's heart sank and yet she didn't know why she even cared. So what if he was to marry. "Who is she trying to have Mr. McPherson marry?" Forcing a smile, Johanna swallowed hard. She felt a bit weak and she began to feel a cold sweat tingle her body. She looked up toward the pale gray storm clouds that began to form and tried to stop her eyes from tearing. Why it was affecting her was perplexing.

"Kathleen? She is a friend of the family. She has had feelings for him since they were kids. Maybe someday he will settle down and have a family, although he proclaims he wants to go where he pleases without any ties, any responsibilities to anyone," announced Jacob with a slight grin.

"That sounds like something he would say," Johanna said with a harsh tone, lifting her head in a prideful stance.

Jacob followed her back to the cabin holding the stack of wood he collected. He tried to hold back his laugh at Johanna's observation and her prideful manner.

Turning to Jacob once again, she asked in almost a whisper, "Does he love her?"

"McPherson? Ah, he loves every woman and they love him too," said Jacob. He noticed her emerald eyes had now turned glossy as if she were about to cry, even though she tried desperately to hide it. Jacob sighed and then rested his hand on her shoulder. "Is he getting to you? Are you actually beginning to care for David?"

"Oh no, absolutely not, I don't care in the least. I have much higher standards, Mr. Evans. Besides he is so, so, difficult," She stated as she gained control of her emotions once again.

"And you are not?" Jacob laughed.

Rain began to sprinkle down on them and Jacob and Johanna continued their trip back to the cabin.

"And where the hell have you two been?" David asked angrily in a way that made them both feel like they were kids being scolded by a parent.

"We went to gather wood for the fire." Jacob answered quickly before Johanna could speak.

"Do you have a problem with that?" Johanna glared.

"As a matter of fact I do," he scowled, "there are footprints outside that do not belong to any of us. Someone knows we're here we need to leave immediately."

David grabbed her arm forcing her towards him and stared down at her. "Listen little girl, you could be in danger, you need to stop acting like a child, and listen to me for once."

"No, you could be in danger. Let go of my arm." Johanna said gritting her teeth and pulling away. "I'm tired of you treating me terribly. Don't touch me, don't talk to me, and don't even look at me." Johanna reached for the doorknob.

"Where do you think you're going?" David yelled after her as if she were a child being scolded.

"Out!" she screamed back, slamming the door behind her, thunder cracked adding to the drama, and she stepped into the pouring rain which now fell like autumn leaves in a gusty breeze.

"It's raining; you're going to catch the death of yourself." David bit his lip. "I guess I better go get her, you'll never know what kind of trouble she'll get herself into." He left without looking at Preston and Jacob's blank expressions as they watched the scene before them unfold.

Johanna's silken body was now drenched, the dampness had cooled her hot head and she raised her hands above her head to feel the freedom she felt out in the open. The heavy beats of the rain pounding the ground drowned out David's voice calling for her. When she finally did hear him, she ducked behind a tree so he'd pass.

"Johanna?" he yelled again this time in a concerned and frantic tone. The rain now poured harder, but beyond the splashing rain he heard a faint giggle. Turning he saw the most beautiful woman he had ever laid eyes on. Her golden hair clinging to her face, dress and petticoat beneath stuck to her so tightly it showed her full figure, and that smile, that teasing smile, seductively invited him to her.

David grinned taking a closer step. He lifted his hand to her cheek and pulled away her wet hair that hid her emerald eyes. What was it about her that made him feel so alive? He felt anger and passion at once. She was a child but everything about her was a woman.

"Do you really hate me?" David asked her with a slight grin.

"No, I do not," she admitted and then held her breath. Her gaze locked on his. She wanted desperately to remove herself from his powerful presence. He had an undeniable power over her that made her want more of him. She hated him for it. It was hard for her to swallow. His handsome face gazing upon hers made Johanna tremble. The look on his face made it even harder for her to turn away. He looked at her with wonder as if he had never seen her before.

"Do you treat all your prisoners like this, Lieutenant?" asked Johanna, trying desperately to break their intense moment.

"Only the ones who are defiant," said David. "Of course, until they are broken."

Johanna stared him down. "Are you saying that I am a horse or child?" she asked.

"Does it matter?" he asked.

Johanna was so furious with David she could actually feel her blood pressure boil, and her face burn with anger, but she could not make any words form. She stared at him. Watching him laugh at her was painful. She had let down her guard for some odd reason. Why she did continued to perplex her.

Johanna turned in anger and tried to step away from him to head back to the cottage.   Before she took another step, David grabbed her arm and turned her toward him with a jerk.

They were now face to face again, staring in each other's eyes, inches from each other. Another crack of thunder and a flash of lightening outlined their circumstance. A small stream began to form nearby that had been created by the downpour of rain.

Johanna tried to push him away although he was too strong for her. His fists wrapped around her wrists, she tried to struggle, but her heart wanted to give in. David whispered her name calming her. "Johanna," he whispered.

Her face felt hot again but it wasn't because of anger. She froze and looked up into his handsome face.

He whispered her name again, "Johanna."

She was entranced, it was as if the whole world had stopped, became motionless, as if there was no rain, no war, and no cares. Time had held on and wouldn't tick to the next second.

David's mind couldn't comprehend what he was seeing. Even wet with the rain pouring over her, Johanna was the most beautiful woman he had ever seen. He whispered her name as if it was a heavenly secret he unveiled.

"Johanna," he said once again. She wanted him even though she struggled, he knew. He could see it in her eyes. He felt it he was consumed by it, by her. She was intoxicating. He had lost. He could not pretend anymore. He had to have her. He would never be the same again. It was then, in that moment, that space in time that the revelation came. Lieutenant David McPherson knew that he loved her.

David's eyes traced Johanna's lips, he wanted to taste them, feel their warmth, their tenderness. His hands shook as they began to touch her silken face. He feared if he touched her, she'd disappear into the night as if in a dream. He could not wait any longer he had to kiss her, and with a powerful embrace, his lips collided with hers.

Chapter 6

*A*fter that day Johanna couldn't remember much about the incident with David. The moment they had shared together was a blur. It seemed more like a dream. She could hardly remember when Private Graystone whisked her away from David. They were interrupted by unexpected arrival of Malcolm. He had knocked David out with his revolver with one swift blow. David had no idea what hit him until it was too late.

David and Johanna didn't hear Malcolm approach

them from behind with the downpour of rain and the crashing thunder. As David fell to the ground it was there in that instant, Malcolm took her. He grabbed her, covered her mouth, and before she could scream, he whispered in her ear.

"Colonel Lee has sent me," said Malcolm. "I am here to save you. Please don't scream or there will be blood spilled this night."

That was enough for Johanna. She never said a word. And they rode back toward Charleston and she never looked back, not once. A blur, her time with David was something that changed her. But it was just a blur.

Private Graystone and Johanna didn't speak until arriving at her home where her uncle had sent soldiers to keep watch. She entered, bathed, changed clothes, and went down into the dining room where Malcolm and dinner sat waiting for her. There were also at least a dozen servants she didn't recognize milling around.

It was hard for Johanna to smile, but she knew that the soldier was doing his job. She couldn't be angry with him.

"Thank you," she forced a smile, "you saved my life."

"Miss Lee, I was sent to take you to Arlington. I don't really know what happened when you were abducted," Malcolm looked at her with concern, "I know that Union soldier tried to force himself on you out there, and I am sorry that I wasn't here sooner. I will never forgive myself for staying at the inn and not coming straight here."

Johanna looked up at him with confusion and then frowned. "I just want to forget all about it," she lied.

"On Sunday, I will take you to Arlington as planned. In the mean time, your uncle left word that he would like us to stay and meet him at the Beauregard's party in two evenings from now." Malcolm smiled. "I would love to take you." He asked in a charming plea even Johanna couldn't turn down.

"I thought he couldn't meet us?" questioned Johanna.

"A change of plans," answered Malcolm.

Johanna couldn't think of anything she would rather not do, but she half smiled back and said, "That would be nice, thank you Mr. Graystone."

"Please call me Malcolm," he noticed her somber tone

and put his hand on hers. "Cheer up Miss Johanna, it will be fun, I promise."

The next day she spent in her room with thoughts of David and how she began to notice his kindness more during their time together. She was confused by her feelings. He was her captor, he was arrogant, yet, he made her feel an unbelievable shock to her heart every time he would lay his eyes on her or touch her. She was torn between hate and love. One second she despised him and the other she didn't know how she would go on without him. It was ridiculous. She was being ridiculous she thought. How could this infatuation be good? It was not like her to feel such emotions. She must be coming down with something. She felt her face. Oh yes, it was flushed, she must be ill. Maybe she would lie down some more she thought.

"Stop thinking about him," she angrily whispered to herself. She tried to read and then realized she left her magazine with the Union soldiers. She was heartbroken. How could she get it back?

She could not live with knowing that they had

something that was so precious to her, unfortunately, they were long gone. They had what they needed. She knew they must have found her uncle's cigar box with the plans inside.

Then she smiled to herself and put her hand on the locket that caressed her neck. She was able to save one page of her uncle's plans, the map. They might have some of it, but they didn't have all of it.

"Now go back to your regiment and see if your big heroes!" She actually had a twinge of sadness for them. They would look like idiots with half of a plan. She could hear someone at the front door. She hid her locket back in her dress and looked once again in the mirror and dashed down the stairs to see who had visited her.

# # #

"Damn!" said David punching the ground. He was angry and humiliated by his surprised blow to the head. It took him awhile to awaken when Jacob called his name and helped him off the ground.

"Are you okay?" Jacob said helping David with a hand up. "That bump on your head looks painful."

"She's gone," David said as he felt his goose egg. His gaze directed past Jacob, looking in the direction Johanna had disappeared. There were footprints in the mud that lay before them. It had proven she had not escaped on her own.

"I know. I think we need to reevaluate what we are going to do. We have to get out of here before recruits come," said Jacob. "You know she has the map with her, don't you? Preston was admiring her locket earlier and she refused to let him look in it. It must be in there. The good news is we still have the cigar box we found in the liquor cabinet. I think it's more important than just a bunch of exquisite cigars."

Preston finally joining them with one of the cigars in his mouth, "Yeah, these cigars are going to determine who wins the war," he laughed.

David still looking around as if Johanna was going to appear out of the woods ignored the men, "I blew it. I stopped thinking about the mission for one second. I know better. I have to get her back," said David.

"What do you mean? Have you gone mad?" asked Preston.

"Yes..." David hesitated and then caught himself, "no, I just mean, we need to get that map from her."

"Right, how do you suppose we do that?" Jacob asked.

"I don't know yet," said David still rubbing his head.

"Well, I am in, whatever you decide," said Preston.

"Thanks, I appreciate your support," said David.

Preston laughed, "No, it's not that, I am just amused by the effect Miss Lee has on you."

# # #

When Malcolm met Johanna at her door to escort her to the Beauregard's ball, she was surprised to notice how very handsome he was. He had a boyish charm about him that made a girl's heart skip a beat in his presence.

"You look lovely," he smiled at her and helped her

into the carriage. "It's hard for me to take my eyes off you." Johanna blushed not used to the attention. "What, you don't believe me?"

"Thank you. It's been a long time since anyone has noticed," smiled Johanna still blushing.

"I find that hard to believe. You are the most beautiful woman I have ever laid eyes upon." He continued with his compliments.

"Be careful Mr. Graystone, I might skip the ball and take you straight to church," smiled Johanna.

"Only if it's for our wedding," he said with a grin. They both laughed. Johanna slightly embarrassed.

Johanna looked out the carriage window smiling and thinking how she couldn't wait to see the look on Clarice's face when she walked in on the arm of a handsome man that Clarice hadn't yet had her hands on.

Johanna had history with Clarice Beauregard. They unfortunately belonged in the same society. Johanna had to be exposed to her for teas, dinners, and of course for balls. Johanna found her to be mean and manipulative. Normally Clarice didn't bother her in the least, especially because her family most of the time resided in New Orleans.

But when circumstance would have it and Johanna had to see her, she would make every effort not to encourage Clarice's manner. She wasn't worth the effort.

Clarice was the model of what every man wanted. She was beautiful, seductive, and charismatic. Johanna had to learn this lesson first hand. She was in the wake of Clarice's power she held over men. One young man Johanna thought had potential to be a suitor was ruined by Clarice. More like ruined him. She set her sights on him and devoured him with one swift blow. Johanna was in the crossfire and was also burned. From that day on, Johanna vowed to never ever be involved with any man that Clarice had encountered. It was a no win situation. He would forever be regretful of losing Clarice or regretful of never getting the chance.

Johanna sighed with a heavy heart. Just a small glimpse of heartache always brought Johanna to that place where she felt that pang of deception. The carriage listed to the right and with it brought Johanna out of her sharp and painful past.

"Are you all right?" Malcolm questioned her hardened look.

"Oh yes. I am not quite enthusiastic for parties they give me a bit of anxiety." She answered.

"Well, there is nothing to fear. I shall not leave your side." Malcolm smiled.

Johanna smiled a not so convincing smile back.

Chapter 7

ntering the ballroom took Johanna's breath away. She had been to parties before and they always made her gasp. The scene was a portrait picture of beautiful ladies dressed in their best gowns for the sole purpose of impressing the handsome Citadel cadets that filtered the room. Her senses were bombarded with the smell of tobacco and perfume and music that filled the air. While the musicians played she watched gentlemen approach ladies for their hand at a dance.

Southern Beauty

"This is how gentlemen treat ladies," she whispered to herself but aimed at David. She had to smile. This was what the South was all about. What made Southerners complete, what they prided themselves on, hospitality, celebration, and enjoying ones company, she thought to herself. Except, Clarice was here, the evil Clarice, and to top it off, it was her family's ball.

"I'll go get us some drinks to cool us off," Malcolm smiled at her and disappeared into the scenery. Her eyes searched the room for her uncle. She could hear the conversation next to her.

"Can you believe it? Rene Beauregard is here and so is the cadet that shot at the Star of the West, George Edward," said a young lady to her friends.

"Rene is so handsome," said another.

"Oh, this is the best ball ever! Look at all the handsome cadets," said another giddy young lady.

Johanna decided to remove herself from the gossiping girls into another room which seemed to be abandoned of party goers. It was the Beauregard's drawing room. She noticed a painting on the wall and out of curiosity and

75

boredom decided to examine it closer.

"That was my grandmother's from Paris," Johanna surprised by the intrusion, looked in the direction of the speaker.

"Oh, Mr. Beauregard, you startled me," Johanna said.

Please call me Rene," he said with a slight bow.

His smile and his presence were a powerful combination, the effect it had on Johanna made her slightly blush.

Johanna had never been introduced to Rene. He had always been shielded by Clarice and away for schooling. She definitely understood what the fuss was all about. He was tall and extremely handsome. Maybe too handsome, she thought to herself. She slightly smiled and looked around the room, realizing they were now alone.

"I fear I do not know who you are, and I thought I knew all the beautiful ladies in Charleston," said Rene in his charming Cajun accent.

"You mean you courted every beautiful lady in Charleston," said Johanna, not ready to smile yet.

This made him laugh. "I am not that bad, New

Orleans maybe. Are you friends with Clarice?"

"Hardly," she whispered. I am here for my uncle."

"And who pray tell is your uncle?" asked Rene intrigued.

She scanned the room once again nervously. "I should go."

He followed her glance. "Oh, you don't want to be caught seen with me," he asked.

"A lady should never be alone with a man she does not know," she said.

"Well, it appears you knew my name," Rene smiled, "therefore you must know me."

"Everyone knows of you Mr. Beauregard, and your reputation with young ladies," Johanna said in an accusing tone.

This made him laugh again. Johanna couldn't believe how charming he was when he laughed. It made her smile.

"Very well then, I will only let you pass if you tell me one thing," he said with a grin.

"And what is that Mr. Beauregard?" Johanna asked.

"Your name," Rene said.

# # #

"David, do you think this is going to work?" asked Jacob.

"Absolutely, I just need you to meet me with the horses," David said. "Preston, ride ahead and secure a place for us for the night. Use every contact that you can muster. We need this to work."

"Don't let that beauty fool you again," warned Preston. "You know she distracted you out there so the soldier could attack you."

"I know. I won't let it happen again," David more determined to finish his mission and be done with Johanna for good.

"Those are the most dangerous, the pretty ones. They like to spin you in their web and then attack without warning," Preston smiled.

"I am no Yankee fool, Preston," David angrier thinking about Johanna's deception.

Jacob looked at David's determined look on his face, "I think she must have been as surprised as we all were."

"Then why would she leave me unconscious, I could have been dead for all she knew," David gritted his teeth.

"We did hold her prisoner. Maybe she didn't have a choice," Jacob trying to give Johanna, who he had grown fond of, the benefit of the doubt.

David frowned at the thought, "There's always a choice. She made hers. Now I am making mine."

# # #

Johanna left Rene alone in the drawing room and once again searched another room for her uncle or any signs of where Malcolm disappeared too.

"There you are, I thought you found another man to escort you," Malcolm came up behind Johanna and handed her a cool drink.

"Oh thank you. I am just taking all this in. I never thought I would say this, let alone think it, but I believe I just might miss all of this," she said.

"There will be other balls to go to in Virginia," Malcolm said.

"I know, but it won't be quite the same," she said.

"Well it could be if you let me escort you to every one of them." He smiled at her, that adorable smile that made a dimple form on his cheek. She tried to ignore his comment.

"Sometimes I feel like everyone is staring at us. Do you feel the same?" He glanced around the room and noticed a group of young ladies were whispering and gawking at them.

"No, not at all," he looked back at Johanna.

She smiled back at him.

"Oh, there is Rene. I would like you to meet him, he's a good friend of mine," said Malcolm.

"Oh, but I have already." It was too late. Malcolm pulled her in Rene's direction without waiting for Johanna's answer.

"Rene, it's great to see you," Malcolm shook his hand.

"Malcolm, thought you were with the North and Lee?" Rene questioned with a smile.

"Oh I am, with Lee that is. I actually have taken on a new assignment for him," he looked down at Johanna. "Meet my new charge, Johanna Lee."

"Oh, we have met earlier. I think I scared her off though, she wouldn't tell me her name," Rene smiled at Johanna triumphantly. "I know it now."

"Hands off Rene, there are plenty of women here to choose from and Miss Lee is not one of them."

Rene laughed. Johanna was extremely uncomfortable with the men who were talking to each other as if she was not in attendance.

"Excuse me, I am going to see a friend I just noticed across the room," and Johanna gracefully yet quickly left their presence.

She couldn't believe men behaved this way, and she couldn't believe they were behaving this way towards her. No one ever paid attention to her like this. Not ever. It was a mix of excitement and one of confusion. She hadn't really seen a friend; she just needed to get away. She thought maybe air would help her clear her head.

Johanna gazed into the moonlit sky as she stood on

the balcony overlooking the garden. She could hear the whispers of ladies gossiping about Rene's good looks and wondering if he would show up at all since he had left West Point. Johanna laughed to herself about the nonsense of women. Little did they know if they would actually go into the ballroom they would find him there searching for his new conquest.

She focused on the music playing behind her in the ballroom where Malcolm was left a moment ago with Rene chatting like school boys. A soft breeze tickled the nape of her neck. Her heart never feeling such conflicting emotions, David was on her mind again. She closed her eyes and began to think back of the moment he had kissed her. It seemed so long ago, but in reality only a couple of days. Where had he gone? Had he felt it too? There was no moment of the day that went by that she didn't think of him. He probably went back to his family, to his life without her, to the girl his mother wanted him to marry. She wouldn't even entertain the thought of him being dead from Malcolm's blow.

"No," she thought, "I will not ruin my sweet

memories of a stolen moment with disappointing realism." She willed herself to only think of the most romantic experience she had ever had, the only romantic experience she had ever had. And the sad thing was it was someone with she vowed to hate. She kept her eyes shut to bring the moment closer to her, David closer to her. And then she heard a voice of familiarity.

"Southern Beauty, my head still hurts from the knockout kiss you gave me," David said.

Johanna's eyes fluttered open, but she was too afraid to turn around. Was this her imagination or was David behind her? She stared into the heavens silently praying he was indeed standing behind her, yet conflicted with feeling afraid for her uncle. She held her breath, and she gripped onto the railing of the balcony with her gloved hand to prevent herself from falling, for her legs felt like they were going to buckle beneath her.

David walked up to her, afraid to touch her for she might disappear like his reoccurring dreams of her. I love her. I love her. His hand slowly reached her shoulder, hesitating, and then put it down again at his side.

The men had been keeping their eye on Johanna from afar. There were times when David planned his approach, but the opportunity to be alone with her seemed wouldn't present itself. When scoping the town, David's luck changed when a young lady invited him to a ball. While the men had kept an eye on Johanna, David spent his time playing up to his new interest to make sure Johanna was included in the invitation. The night of the ball, the men decided to warn David of her new relationship with a southern soldier blossoming, which included meals together and reading books by the fireplace. The soldier seemed to never leave her side. David was already angry with her. Had that moment in the rain not meant anything? Had the entire time they were together mean nothing to her?

David was alarmed to find that this same man had escorted her to the ball. He wondered if it was that easy for her to move on to another suitor. Maybe if she knew that after he came out of unconsciousness, he and his men followed in a frantic pace to retrieve her. He kept thinking. And then he caught himself once again. "What am I saying? I am not a suitor. I am only after the map. She is a vixen, a siren in disguise. She tricked me. How could I feel anything for her?"

He whispered in her ear, he broke the silence, "My precious Southern Beauty, I waited an eternity to be with you, may we never part again." David wanted to say but couldn't. Instead he made himself cold and agitated, "You will no longer be in the way. You either produce that map, or your uncle dies tonight."

He handed her the Blackwood's Magazine although he still had in his possession the cigar box.

Johanna had never heard him so angry before. She felt frightened. "Oh David," she gasped and turned to face him, "I waited so long. Is it really you?" She would not dare say what she was thinking. So she stepped away quietly, and looked him over. "What are you doing here?" She was surprised by his attire. He was not wearing his Union uniform, but a new Confederate one. "You didn't convert did you?" She questioned with raised eyebrows.

He couldn't help but laugh at her observation and her question. It broke the tension between them and the seriousness of the moment.

"Never, do you think they would let me in here wearing mine? I would have been shot on sight. Besides, I just got friendly with a young lady in town and she invited me. She is a little persistent." He flashed a confident smile, with an almost arrogant stance.

"A young lady?" she questioned a little taken back.

"You might know her?" He asked, still trying to gauge her.

Johanna swallowed hard as her heart plunged. "No, I probably do not. Everyone I know has too much self-respect to even want to come within ten feet of you." She looked at him accusingly.

"Ahh," thought David, he hit a sore spot with her, she does care about me. So he continued, "Well, it didn't take much to charm her. She seems to like men in uniform."

Johanna didn't answer. She was seething with jealousy.

"Anyway, she is very pretty. I think she wants to introduce me to her father? Isn't that crazy?" David kept trying to push her into some kind of emotion.

This was unbelievable she thought to herself.

Johanna couldn't trust what she was hearing. Who could this girl be? Had he not felt anything? Who was this mysterious woman? She couldn't think of this anymore, it hurt too much. She felt like she had been punched in the stomach. She looked at him in disgust.

Her temperature rising along with her voice, "Why did you come here?" She decided it was best to ignore his ramblings. It only hurt her more and ruined the only remembrance she had of romance that wasn't written in a book.

David knew he must have gone too far, so he tried to backtrack and get back the look in her eyes when she first saw him, but it was too late. She stood in a cold stance and continued her glare.

"I'm sorr," he was trying to apologize but she interrupted him.

"Well, it seems you have found some other poor girl to use to get what you wanted. What did it take, a day to move on or a couple of hours?" Did she just say that aloud? Johanna surprised herself. "Why did you even come back here?" Johanna tried desperately to hold back her tears, but when one slipped down her frosted cheek, she turned towards the garden once more. David was about to touch her hand and bring it towards him, when a man suddenly interrupted them.

"Miss Johanna, is this man bothering you?" Malcolm Graystone came out onto the balcony, interrupting what it looked like, a lover's quarrel. Johanna cleared her eyes and turned to him.

"No Mr. Graystone. I'm fine," she said.

"I'm sorry, and you are?" he inquired toward David, who still hadn't turned in Malcolm's direction until now. David nodded. Malcolm's eyes widened and then he composed himself with a smile. He turned to Johanna. "May I have the next dance?"

"Yes, I would like that, thank you." And she passed David and held Malcolm's arm toward the dance floor. She couldn't look back. She was mortified she had given away her secret jealousy. On the dance floor Malcolm interrogated Johanna.

"Who was the gentleman?" Malcolm asked.

"He was no gentleman," she said. "He was the one

you bashed in the head with your gun, and now I would like to do it myself," she wanted to say. Instead she lied. "Just someone who was sure of himself that I would be interested in a dance, I guess he didn't want to take no for an answer." She had no idea why she continued to protect him.

"I see, how quite peculiar," said Malcolm.

"What's that?" asked Johanna.

"Oh, he looks familiar," he said, "but I am not quite sure where from."

"I know why he looks familiar to you," she thought. They were interrupted by General P.G.T. Beauregard himself.

"Hello, Private Graystone, it's so nice to see you again. I see you've retrieved the package," he looked at Johanna and smiled.

Malcolm smiled back and excused himself from Johanna to make it a private conversation.

"Oh, my delivery is not quite complete, but I am sure the package will be delivered in a few weeks time. I am confident that my goals will be achieved by the end of the delivery," said Malcolm.

Not interested in their conversation anyway, Johanna made her way across the room. She felt considerable relief when she spied her dear friend Mary Alice.

"You have truly surprised me! It's so nice to see you out." Mary Alice hugged her. "I can't believe you would come to Clarice's ball."

"It's not her ball it's her family's ball. Actually, I came with someone," Johanna pointed to Malcolm who had been still involved in conversation with Beauregard. "He's over there."

"I guess you don't need me to set you up, you did fine on your own," Mary Alice laughed impressed with her friend's companion for the evening. "Where did you find him, and does he have a brother?"

"Oh, he came and rescued me from a terrible situation and a dreadful man," said Johanna.

"You must tell," Mary Alice intrigued now.

"Another time Mary Alice, I must find my uncle. Have you seen him yet?" Johanna asked.

"No, not yet, but I will let you know if I do. Did you hear that Clarice's mysterious lover is here at the party? I haven't seen him yet, but I heard he is the most handsome man in the room." She looked at Johanna's agitated state. "Of course until you came with Mr. Graystone."

Johanna smiled back at her. "You are truly a good friend, Mary Alice."

"Oh no, she is heading this way," said Mary Alice.

"Who is?" By the time Johanna glanced away to see who was approaching them, Mary Alice slipped away.

"Hello Johanna," Clarice said with a bit of arrogance.

"Ah, Clarice," Johanna nodded with a slight bow.

"It's so nice to see you out," Clarice lied. "It's been awhile."

"Well, thank you, you have a lovely home." Johanna followed.

"It's not as nice as the one in New Orleans, but it is charming. It is Parisian decor. You probably recognized it, actually, you probably feel more at home here. Anyway, I am surprised to see you." Clarice said.

"Oh?" Johanna questioned ignoring Clarice's jab about her family.

"Well, since you have been in that little depression of

yours, secluded from everyone, a lot has happened." Clarice said.

"A lot has happened where?" questioned Johanna.

"Oh, not with the conflict, I don't waste my time on depressing thoughts like that, it would ruin one's day, don't you think? No, I mean a lot has happened to me." Clarice proudly announced.

Oh great, here she goes, thought Johanna.

"Yes?" Johanna asked although she didn't want to know, equally annoyed with Mary Alice for leaving her stuck with Clarice and her nonsensical talk.

"Oh yes. You might not have heard yet," she steps closer and lowers her voice to a whisper," but I am soon to be engaged."

"Engaged!?" Johanna gasped.

"Keep your voice down. My papa doesn't know yet," Clarice said.

Stumbling over her words, still in shock, "You committed to only one?" Johanna mockingly asked.

Clarice laughs. "Oh, it is very easy when you're in love. I am sure you someday you will know what I mean."

Clarice slams Johanna.

"Who could he possibly be?" Johanna now extremely annoyed by her remarks.

"Oh, you wouldn't know him, he is new to the regiment," said Clarice.

"A soldier?" Johanna choked on her words.

"Oh yes. I only just met him but he and I knew right away we were meant to be together." Clarice announced with pride.

"That's so nice for you." Johanna said with slight sarcasm.

"I am sure you will be invited to our wedding," said Clarice.

"Oh, thank you very much. I will look forward to it." Johanna lied.

"Please do not tell anyone what I've told you. I want us to tell my papa tonight. I guess there really isn't anyone for you to tell is there? I have more guests to talk to so I must leave you, goodbye." Clarice gets one more jab in.

"He's here?" Johanna asked in vain. Clarice had already begun to mingle and gossip with the other guests.

Johanna cannot figure why she would be so interested in finding who this new soldier is in Clarice's life. For some reason it vexed her. She wanted to know who he was. Who would possibly trust her? He must not know her very well.

"She is truly evil isn't she?" Mary Alice stepped back into Johanna's sight.

"Thanks a lot," said Johanna.

Mary Alice laughed, "I knew you could handle her yourself. You always could."

"Can you believe the nerve of her? She truly thinks she is the only one that has ever been in love," said Johanna.

"Are you in love Johanna?" Mary Alice questioned.

Chapter 8

*D*avid walked to the edge of the balcony looking over the garden's edge. He pondered his dilemma. He wanted to express his love to Johanna, but his mission was clouding his focus. Or was his love for Johanna clouding his mission? He didn't know anymore. Maybe I should tell her I love her. I don't know if she would even believe me. Oh no…what am I doing? His thoughts were interrupted.

"Hello my sweet Lieutenant." David knew that voice,

and he closed his eyes to wish her away but she came closer. She grabbed his hand and turned him around towards her. Pressing herself against him she whispered, "What are you doing out here in the shadows? Were you waiting for me?" asked Clarice.

She was hoping David would enjoy her playfulness. David found it to be revolting, he found her to be revolting. He was truly surprised that a woman with her upbringing would have such a strong, straight forward personality when in the presence of a gentleman. It was down right disgraceful and a bit shocking. Although he understood why men would fall for her hard and fast, she was flawlessly beautiful. Her body was curvy and she wore her gowns well. It also helped that she came from a very powerful and wealthy family. She was confidant enough to know what she wanted and not afraid to go after it even if it meant pretending to be a bashful lover if that is what it took. Her mastery of manipulation was evident the more time David spent with her. She had a gift. It was a dangerous gift, but she knew when to use it to her advantage every time.

David was never taken in by her. He was never

fooled by her outer appearance for her inner beauty was much to be desired and that was something she apparently could not hide. She had been the perfect cover for his covert operation to get to Johanna and now he did not need her friendship any longer so he thought.

"I have to tell you something," he tried to stop her.

"Tell me later, let's go be together alone somewhere," she insisted.

"Now?" David asked out of shock.

"You seem surprised?" she asked grinning seductively.

"I just…" he tried to say, but she quickly leaned in to him and before he could protest, she kissed him hard upon the lips.

# # #

Johanna saw Malcolm heading toward her and she was surprised that she was actually blushing. Over the course of just a few days they had spent much time together.

She had unexpectedly begun to feel fondly toward him, and since the party she was actually a bit impressed with him. While he sauntered over to her, his face beamed and he stared at her like she was the only one in the room. Now any woman would feel important with that kind of attention, Johanna thought. Malcolm was a genius at making you feel like you were the most important person in the world. Johanna liked that about him and was also weary of him for it.

"Miss Johanna, I was told your uncle has arrived and has stepped out onto the balcony. Should we go see him?" Malcolm smiled pleased with himself.

"The balcony, are you sure?" Johanna feared for her uncle's safety, that is where they had left David alone. She ran ahead of Malcolm leaving Mary Alice behind.

Her heart beat faster, she was to reunite with her uncle and maybe even David, who she still was conflicted about.

Once David came in view Johanna was mortified to see him in a compromising scene with Clarice. Johanna's heart stopped. She was horror-struck. As Johanna ran back into the ballroom where the music played merrily and the couples danced with delight, she ran into Malcolm who had been lagging behind.

"Was he not there?" he asked.

"No," was all Johanna could muster.

"Oh, I must have been mistaken." Malcolm smiled in triumph and then quickly noticed her agitated state. Feeling a tinge of regret he said, "Are you okay?"

"I am fine," she lied. "I want to leave now. I want to go to Virginia tonight."

"But, this is a party let's have fun, maybe we should dance again." And before Johanna could speak, Malcolm pulled her on the ballroom floor. Johanna could barely breathe or think straight. She tried to smile at Malcolm but couldn't stop thinking about what she had seen. Thankful her uncle was not in danger but horrified at finding David kissing Clarice. It was a blow she felt she could never recover from.

"May I cut in?" David interrupted their dance. Malcolm didn't utter a word or put up a fight, he was so shocked to see the redhead he met just a few weeks earlier standing right in front of him in a beautiful crimson gown ready to take his hand for a dance.

"No, I don't think so," Johanna gritted her teeth, but it was too late. The mesmerized Malcolm had already left her side for Clarice.

"Now what is wrong?" David asked as he bowed.

Johanna not wanting to make a scene curtsied back. She was so mortified that her heart was actually breaking. Even though it all made sense, he must have been Clarice's lover, them soon to be engaged, and to find him molesting her on the balcony it just put a knife in her chest.

"I see you found your Southern whore" Johanna straightened herself up. She refused to let him bother her anymore. She began to hate him. She must have been mistaken about her affection towards him.

"Oh, but you are my Southern Beauty," he whispered in her ear.

"Just stay away from me," surprising herself, her lips quivered as she whispered, but she did not cry.

"I can't," he said more with feeling than he wanted to express. If he would have said what was on his heart, his words would have freed her from the pain.

"I need that map. Your uncle has arrived and being held by Preston with a gun pointed to his chest."

Johanna's face went pale. She searched the party with her eyes trying to find her uncle, trying to find Preston. She looked back at David.

"Why are you doing this to me?" Johanna couldn't remember ever being this confused in her entire life. Everything had always seemed black and white to her, right or wrong. She couldn't take this emotional mountains and valleys he was sending her on. One minute she wanted him desperately, the next she never wanted to see him again. She wanted to throw the locket at him and be done.

"He's on your side the last time I checked," Johanna said with conviction.

"Then why is he in enemy territory?" David asked.

"He still has friends here," Johanna insisted.

"I need that map," he said.

"I don't have it here. I left it at the mansion. I will take you there. Just leave him alone," She was desperate and realized now she loathed him even more. He tried to grab her locket that was peeking out of her dress. "It's not in there anymore," she lied smacking his hand away.

"As soon as I get that map he will be released. And if you so desire, you and I will say our goodbyes forever," he said.

"Nothing would give me greater pleasure," she gritted her teeth.

"Do you hate me that much?" he asked.

"Ever since you came into my life you have done nothing but given me heartache," she said in anger.

He was surprised by her words again. Her words were like ice. He wanted to take her in his arms and love her madly and forever. He slipped her into an adjacent room that was deserted.

"What do you mean by that? You know I never meant to hurt you," David needed her to know. "Do I have to remind you? You betrayed me. You made me believe you wanted to kiss me so your rescuer could assault me, how clever you are."

"I didn't know he was there," Johanna confessed.

They gazed upon each other with mixed feelings of

love and loathing. He leaned in closer. He had to kiss her, he had to have her. He loved her so much. He felt like his heart was going to burst.

She didn't know why he was tormenting her. He looked at her with intense love in his eyes. How could this man do this to her? She had given away so much with her silly jealousy. But despite all her anger, she wanted his kiss, his touch. She didn't want to admit it to herself, but she loved him so much it hurt. Inches away from one another, they could feel their breaths colliding, their hearts pounding. He kissed her madly. She let him.

"I...I can't do this," she confessed as she halted their passionate moment. Johanna then ran off into the crowded ballroom, escaping her desire for David.

# # #

David stunned by their steamy passionate kiss and then her quick change of heart left him frozen in place. His hesitancy left him no time to retrieve her before she disappeared into the crowd.

"What happened to you?" Mary Alice noticed how Johanna seemed flushed and a little out of sorts.

"I must be coming down with something." Johanna whispered holding her forehead and feeling her hot cheeks.

"Well, you will be happy to know that Rene has been asking about you," said Mary Alice with excitement.

Johanna didn't say anything, her head and heart still spinning from the encounter with David.

"Did you hear me? Rene. Rene Beauregard was asking me about you. What a blessed evening you are having," Mary Alice said.

"More like cursed. I think I am going to be sick," Johanna's heart pumping even faster now, felt like the room was spinning and everyone in it was slowly darkening.

"Oh, Johanna, you're fainting." Mary Alice noticed as Johanna started to fall backwards.

"I got you," Rene was coming up behind Johanna and as perfect timing showed and she fell into his arms.

The crowd was all in a tizzy, especially the ladies near her at the ball. "Can you believe she fainted into Rene's arms?" said one girl.

"I know, she is so lucky, I wish I would have thought of that," said another.

Johanna woke up on the couch in a very familiar room. It was the same room that Johanna and Rene met and David and she kissed.

"Are you okay, Miss Johanna?" asked Rene.

"I am fine, thank you," she tried to smile. "I guess I was a little overwhelmed."

"I guess," Rene smiled back at her. "It seems here we are again alone." He looked around at the emptiness.

"Oh Rene, you stoop this low as to take advantage of a woman in distress?" Johanna smiled.

"No, I never take advantage, I just think of it as opportunity." He smiled wider this time.

"Very funny," she said.

"If I can amuse, I count that as progress," he laughed.

"I am sure you do," she laughed too.

"Now, I am a little disheartened you came here with Malcolm," said Rene.

"He is taking me to Virginia," she said.

"I've heard. Well, I shall miss our encounters. Maybe I will come and visit you," Rene announced.

"Well, you are very welcome, as a friend of course." She insisted.

"Of course," he grinned.

"Every time I turn around you are with someone else. I am feeling a little slighted by you, Miss Lee," Malcolm interrupted her and Rene.

"Well Mr. Graystone, I am still leaving with you," Johanna smiled.

"Would you like to leave now or are you up for more dancing?" Malcolm asked.

"I am not ready to leave quite yet, but dancing is out of the question. I would like to get some fresh air, if you don't mind. I will join you in a minute," she smiled at both men as she headed toward the small balcony.

"I shall meet you in the ballroom then," smiled Malcolm with a slight bow. Then he turned to Rene grabbing his arm leading him to the ballroom. "Let's go Rene. No way am I leaving you alone with Miss Lee again."

Chapter 9

Johanna stepped out into the small balcony adjacent to the drawing room. She just needed to clear her head. What was she doing? She knew she could never let that passion between her and David ignite again. She had to stay away from him. His presence was too strong. She felt helpless every time he stood near her.

"If I just keep my distance I shall be fine. Just keep my distance and don't look at him. Yes, I will not look at him," she insisted. Those green eyes melted her. That was the key, if she just didn't look into his intense gaze. "If I don't look I won't be tempted," she told herself.

"My kiss does make the ladies swoon." David came out of the darkened corner of the balcony. Johanna froze.

"I actually thought I was going to be sick." She clammed back at him.

"Uh huh," he smiled.

Johanna was determined not to look at him. She tried to measure. "If I stay three feet, no five feet from him, I will be fine."

"Is it your goal to kiss a different girl in each room?" she asked still upset with him about Clarice.

"If you so desire, I will go room to room with you," David smiled.

"How dare you," Johanna said appalled.

David laughed at her anger.

"You took advantage of me," she said.

"And how did I do that?" he asked.

"I don't know you just did," she said.

"You didn't stop me, at least not right away," David smiled watching her frustration rise.

"I was confused, I am confused," she said. "You just shouldn't have done that. You have not been kind to me."

"I haven't been kind to you? I think it is you who left me for dead," he reminded her.

"I guess that bump didn't knock any sense into you," Johanna continued. "You have got to be mad! You kidnap me, hold my uncle by gunpoint, and you expect me to be nice to you? You are the one who hasn't any manners. You have no idea how to treat a lady."

"You are a prisoner of war, not a lady I am courting," said David.

"There isn't a war." Johanna snapped back.

"There will be," insisted David.

"What makes you think I won't let everyone here know right now whose side you're really on?" Johanna threatened.

"Because you would never forgive yourself if something happened to the man you love," he said.

"You mean my uncle?" she questioned. He wasn't talking about her uncle.

"You're coming with me now," David gently but

firmly pulled her toward the ballroom and through the crowd of cadets and ladies. Johanna looked around for someone she might know, but it seemed everyone was too busy to notice her and David.

"I can't leave with you, what will people say?" Johanna whispered.

"Whatever do you mean?" David asked.

"If I leave here with you unescorted, people will assume we are to be engaged," she explained as they continued through the crowded ballroom.

"Engaged? Are you insane? To... be... married?" David asked in confusion.

"Is there any other kind?" They both stopped.

"Do you know how frustrating you are?" David said becoming agitated.

"Oh I do so loathe you!" Johanna said frustrated.

"Loathe me? Such harsh words coming from you Miss Lee," David frustrated now.

"You come here and threaten me and my uncle and you think I should not?" Johanna whispers get louder.

David laughs, "Alright, then why don't you get your

friend there to come with you."

"Oh, Clarice is not enough. You want to kiss Mary Alice too? I will not drag her into this," Johanna bit her lip.

"Oh, this is all about Clarice," David smirked at her comment.

"Have you not promised to be in engaged to her this very evening?" Johanna asked.

"Now I am engaged to her?" David even more confused.

"That is what she is telling everyone," Johanna now back to a whisper.

"That I am to be engaged to her?" David questioned.

"Well, she didn't say you by name, but said it was a new soldier," Johanna beginning to realize she is now gossiping.

"So you assumed that it was me?" David now annoyed.

"Well, after I found you two embracing on the balcony," Johanna accused him with more anger than she wanted to show.

"Well Miss Lee, did you also see me brush her off and

tell her I was in love with someone else?" He continued to pull her through the crowded ballroom.

"What?" Johanna tried to stop not sure if she should be thrilled by the news or not.

"Why am I arguing with you about this?" He grabbed her arm and continued through the mingling couples.

"Are you trying to steal my date?" Malcolm asked David.

"Oh you again, don't you have something you ought to be doing?" asked David.

"Do you two know each other?" Johanna continued to switch back looking at both of them. They ignored her.

"Sir, may I have a word with you?" Malcolm stared David down.

"It would be a pleasure," David stared Malcolm back down.

"Excuse us Miss Lee," they both headed toward the door without once glancing at Johanna.

"What was that all about?" Mary Alice noticed Johanna had been left on her own.

"I have no idea," Johanna and Mary Alice watched

the men walk out of their sight.

"Do they know each other?" inquired Mary Alice.

"I don't' think so," answered Johanna confused at the new situation played out in front of her.

"Now this is very exciting! Maybe they are fighting over you. Where is Rene?" Mary Alice looked around the room. "He should be in on this." exclaimed Mary Alice.

Johanna ignored her friend's excitement. "For some odd reason, I don't think it's really about me."

# # #

"You have the audacity to come here and ruin all my plans," Malcolm accused David.

"Ruin your plans? Who are you working for now, Malcolm?" asked David.

"I have special orders to take Lee's niece to Virginia, envious?" Malcolm smiled arrogantly. "What are you doing here?"

"You, you are Johanna's escort? Wait…you're the

mole?" asked David.

Malcolm grinned. "So, I see you are on a first name basis with her? Well, that is too bad, this one is mine. I suggest you leave us alone. You don't want to ruin that squeaky clean reputation of yours by divulging my secret."

"My mission has nothing to do with Miss Lee," David insisted. "You are supposed to be reporting Lee's every move. How can you do that taking her to Virginia?"

"You don't need to worry about that, I have everything under control," said Malcolm.

"Under your control, what are you getting out of this?" David asked.

"I have my orders. I suggest you stay away from Miss Lee," Malcolm warned David.

"How could anyone trust you with their niece?" David asked him.

Malcolm laughed. "You still sore that I left your sister at the altar? I do hope she has gotten over that by now, clearly you haven't."

David ignored his jab and stared him down.

"I want to know why Johanna is so important to

you," Malcolm questioned.

"She's not." David lied.

"Then what do you care if I fancy her or not?" Malcolm now intrigued by David's concern.

"You, you care about her? That is a laugh. What does she have that you are so interested in?" asked David.

"She is a pretty thing isn't she?" stated Malcolm ignoring David's question, while trying to provoke him.

"Just stay away from her. She doesn't need to be hurt by this." David warned.

"Oh, are you becoming noble now? Don't worry, McPherson, by the end of this mission, I will have saved the day and won the girl!"

David couldn't have predicted this. Not only was the man who was spending time with Johanna someone he actually knew. He was Malcolm Graystone. He was on the Northern side pretending he was a wavering patriot following Lee. He was a master of trickery. He hurt his sister and now he was after Johanna. This was grave indeed.

Malcolm had been bent on beating David at everything since they were at West Point together. Malcolm always looked for the next big mission to carry out, the next mountain to climb, and the next goal to achieve without any regard to morality. David had caught Malcolm cheating at West Point and had him expelled. Malcolm never forgave him and went after his sister when he was away for months with General Meade. Now Johanna was caught in the middle of this. He needed to save her. And if Malcolm had any idea how much David loved her, he would never give up. Malcolm would forever ruin her if it would destroy David.

#   #   #

"Johanna, I thought you would want to know, I just overheard G.T. talking with some cadets. Your uncle was delayed and will not be able to make the ball," Mary Alice relayed what she overheard. "There seems to be some talk of conspiracy and it was too dangerous for him to reach Charleston."

"That lying…" Johanna headed toward the stairs.

"Fight! Fight! There are two soldiers fighting in the foyer!" A young cadet yelled out to his schoolmates.

Everyone stopped dancing and headed to see the added entertainment. "Who are they?" another cadet asked.

"You have got to be kidding me," Johanna stopped dead in front of the two men throwing punches at each other. There before her was David and Malcolm acting like school kids with one knocked to the floor and the other shoved into the door. It was broken up by cadets who were standing by, both men bloodied from their battle.

Mary Alice came behind Johanna, "Which one do you choose? I would definitely take Rene, less mess to clean up."

# # #

After David and Malcolm's encounter everyone returned to the party. The orchestra continued to play and guests returned to their rightful places which included dancing, gossiping and drinking.

Before David stepped out of the parlor he was approached again by Malcolm. What David did not know is

Malcolm had seen Johanna watching them carefully by the door.

Malcolm used her eavesdropping on their conversation to his advantage.

"I just want to know one thing?" asked Malcolm holding his hands up in retreat.

David stared him down not sure if he should trust him. He was on guard in case Malcolm was going to sucker punch him when he wasn't ready.

"What is that?" David asked.

"Do you love Miss Lee?" asked Malcolm loud enough for her to hear.

"Absolutely not," denied David. "I will do anything I can for my mission, and that includes pretending my affections."

"Does she think you love her," asked Malcolm.

"Well, if she does she is mistaken," said David. "I am not marrying anyone. As soon as this mission is over, I will be free to go home. Johanna is just a means to an end. Frankly, I don't know how anyone would want to marry her. Her family is disgraceful. Her parents are in Paris completely ruined and her uncle is becoming a traitor to our country. How could anyone think she is good for marrying?"

"I see," said Malcolm smiling in triumph.

Johanna's face went white and her heart sank. He didn't love her. He was appalled by her and her family. These were all things that she had to swallow in five seconds. Ten seconds ago she might have followed him to the ends of the earth. She now had to accept that he had been deceiving her in so many ways. She had to run. She had to get out of the house, get out of the city, she had to disappear and find her family once and for all.

David walked into the ballroom and saw Johanna's friend standing with other young girls laughing. Mary Alice looked up at him in surprise as he walked toward her.

"Perhaps you could direct me to Miss Lee?" He asked in a serious tone, wiping blood from his lip.

"I...don't know where she went," Mary Alice felt his strong presence intimidating. "She ran off after I told her that her uncle had never made it to Charleston."

"You didn't?" David frustrated his bluff was

revealed, "I need to find her now. Will you help me?"

"Sure," she tried to smile. She didn't know why she was helping him. She knew nothing about him, but he was gorgeous, and if he wanted Johanna that was enough for her. She figured Johanna would be thanking her at their wedding. That made her smile widen. Mary Alice and David searched the party to no avail.

# # #

"I seem to keep running into you Miss Lee," Rene smiled.

"Are you following me Mr. Beauregard?" Johanna looked up into his handsome face.

"I just wanted to be near in case you fainted again," he jabbed.

"Very funny," she smirked.

Concerned he asked, "Are you leaving so soon?"

"Yes, I think I am ready to retire for the night. This girl belongs home with a good book in her hand sitting next to a quiet fireplace."

"A good book, you would rather be at home reading a book than being at the Beauregard's ball?" Rene asked appalled.

"You could say that," smiled Johanna.

"Well, I have a problem with you leaving my party," stated Rene.

"Oh. I am sorry. And why is that?" asked Johanna.

"Well, because I have not got my chance to dance with the most beautiful girl here. You are ruining my reputation. You wouldn't want that now would you?" He grabbed her hand gently, kissed it, and walked her to the dance floor before she could protest. Music and laughter once again filled the air.

Johanna was thinking to herself as she stood on the dance floor once again with another handsome man: "What is going on here? For years I have been ignored and unnoticed by every man alive and here I am at this ball, like Cinderella, except I have three, yes, three men biding for my attention. Even if one was only pretending his affections. Am I in someone else's body this month? Maybe I should look in the mirror to see if I am still me."

When the dance was finished she thanked Rene.

Rene kissed her hand again, and said, "Until we meet again, Miss Johanna Lee," He bowed with a slight grin.

Johanna returned the smile and walked toward the entrance where Malcolm stood with her cape and a black eye.

"Are you ready?" He asked with a quiet smile.

"I am, thank you," said Johanna. She looked once again into the ballroom. Ladies still dancing with their handsome escorts, it was a moment she wanted to remember fondly, despite the drama that had come from it earlier. She held Malcolm's arm and headed toward the exit where a coach waited. She continued to feel as if she was in a strange dream even as he helped her into the carriage.

"It's been quite a night, hasn't it, Miss Lee?" Malcolm asked.

Johanna replied, "Yes, quite a night indeed."

Chapter 10

"I can't believe I let her slip through my fingers once again." David frowned.

"I don't think we are going to get this map of Lee's. I think we should face it, Graystone beat us at this one," Jacob grimaced.

"Not if we catch them in New Orleans. We definitely can beat them there by horse," insisted David.

"How do you know they are going to New Orleans?" asked Jacob.

"That's where he is supposed to connect with Lincoln's man. He gives him the map and Malcolm gets his honor and glory," said David.

"How do you know this?" asked Jacob.

"Meade sent word about Malcolm's plans. He asked me to keep an eye on him too, he seems to be a rogue wave, they are questioning his loyalty," said David. "I am not surprised. I could have told them that from West Point." David looked at the men, "So, are you all in?"

"Absolutely not, I think it's time for me to go home." Jacob announced.

"What about you? Are you in?" David asked Preston.

"I love the New Orleans ladies and music. Besides, my brother just moved into town," Preston smiled. "I am definitely in."

"This is madness. Just stop David. You have to let her go. She belongs with her family."

"This isn't about her," denied David. "It's about Lee's map."

"No, the map is a great excuse," sighed Jacob, "but it's about her and Graystone."

"Come on Jacob," said David frustrated, "you know she can't be misled by him. She needs to know the truth and make her own decision. I just can't let her believe that he is a good guy, trustworthy. You know he will hurt her. He just wants her because he thinks I want her."

"You do want her David. She is a smart girl she will figure it out herself. You have to stick with the mission," Jacob said trying to talk sense into him.

"She has the map. That is our mission. Especially since we never found Lee's plans." said David.

"We have the cigar box, we don't need the map. We will get another map," Jacob replied.

"We don't know what's so important about the cigar box except fine cigars. Maybe she can tell us," David sighed finally giving up his excuses.

"I don't know. How do we know she will tell us? She is a stubborn one," said Jacob.

David smiled at Jacob's observation, and then frowned at his loss. David took a deep breath finally deciding it was time to reveal his true feelings.

"I can't lose her," he whispered so only Jacob could here.

Jacob stared at David in disbelief shaking his head in disapproval.

"It's done then," said Jacob, "you have fallen for her after I begged you to stay away."

"It's not that, I just…" David didn't know how to finish his sentence.

"This is no good David. You are entering into dangerous territory, my dear friend," said Jacob. "You could very well be putting our lives at risk."

David and Jacob stared each other down until Jacob finally relented.

"All right then. Let's go get her," sighed Jacob.

David smiled.

# # #

"I still don't understand why we are on a train to New Orleans instead of on a ship to Arlington," Johanna asked Malcolm as they boarded the train trying to accept their new detour.

"I am sorry, Miss Johanna, but our trip to Virginia had to be delayed. Colonel Lee said you must meet him in New Orleans immediately. He said you have something valuable in your possession and that he wants you to personally hand deliver to him while he is visiting Fort Pike," Malcolm explained. "Do you have something valuable?"

"I am not sure," Johanna chose not to elaborate.

"Do you want to tell me what you think it is?" Malcolm asked.

"Well, I had his cigar box before the union men took it from me. I don't know how it could be valuable. I don't think it was that important to divert our destination." Johanna still didn't feel comfortable enough to give Malcolm her trust especially about the map hidden in her locket.

"So the men have it now?" he asked.

"They have the cigar box, but I was able to take something else," she hesitated but mentioned it anyway, "his map."

"I see. What is this map of, do you know?" he asked curious.

"I am not sure. I never really looked at it. I guess it's from the famous balloonist," she was still feeling hesitant divulging information.

"John Steiner? They say he had the only copy, I didn't think it was true," Malcolm's eyes lit up. "Why don't you give it to me so you will no longer be in harm's way? It's probably safer in my hands."

"I don't know," Johanna was weary of him and his excitement. "Why would my uncle send for me and not just his papers?"

"You have a good point," Malcolm said trying not to alarm her. "Maybe it's safer in your hands, especially if the soldiers who kidnapped you didn't get their hands on it."

"Why are Union soldiers after something of my uncle's when he is still part of the Union? Why don't they just ask him for it? And where do you stand in all of this? Are you for the Union or a Confederate?"

"I guess that is a hard question to answer during these tumultuous times," he paused for attention, "let's just say I am on Colonel Lee's side, wherever that may lead me."

"I know what you mean. Well, I am grateful for that. It is so hard to know who to trust anymore." Johanna said still feeling unsure if she should have confided in him.

"I understand," Malcolm smiled. "I hope you know you can trust me."

As the train left the station, Johanna found the rocking sensation had put her to sleep quickly after they boarded. She didn't get much time to speak with Malcolm about their evening the night before. He seemed quieter than usual about it and she didn't feel much like chatting either. They seemed as if they were hung over from the ball, but neither of them drank. Johanna thought to herself, no alcohol, but they had all acted like fools, so really what was the difference.

Johanna was stirred by the sound of papers being shuffled. She almost made herself known until she realized Malcolm was trying to carefully go through her trunk without awakening her and doing a poor job at it.

"What do you think you are doing?" Johanna asked startled by his behavior. Malcolm jumped.

"Here you are," Malcolm pulled out her shawl and placed it over her. "I'm sorry I wasn't trying to go through your things, I just wanted to cover you up. You looked a bit chilly." Malcolm said recovering from his shock of being discovered.

Johanna still not sure of his intentions eyed him over seeing if his actions would give him away.

"Honestly Miss Johanna, I was only trying to take care of you. Please let me at least do that." Malcolm smiled hoping she would ease up on her accusing stare.

"Thank you Mr. Graystone. You are too kind to me." Johanna smiled back decidedly giving him the benefit of the doubt.

"We should be in New Orleans by morning," Malcolm quickly changed the subject. "Have you ever been to New Orleans?"

"No I have not," said Johanna.

"It's an amazing city I hope to show you around while we are there," he paused, "Oh, by the way I have made accommodations for us. I will be staying at the St. Charles Hotel. You on the other hand, I have secured a place with a family on the Garden district. It's with one you might know, a Mrs. Abigail Jenkins?"

"Oh my, with all the craziness, I forgot my dear friend is here," Johanna said pleased at her new accommodations. "Thank you so much! You just made my day," she placed her hand on his and squeezed it gently in a thankful gesture.

"I am glad it is that easy to make you happy," Malcolm said delighted by her touch and pleased with her reaction. "It is my hope that I can make you that happy every day."

Johanna blushed. "Well, I would like to see you try, Mr. Graystone," she said with a hint of playfulness.

"It will be my pleasure I assure you," he smiled revealing his dimples and his charm once again.

"How long do you think we will be staying?" Johanna asked.

"I fear it may be indefinitely, unless we can get Colonel Lee all the items he needs back in his possession," Malcolm replied.

"Oh, I must get to Arlington. What can I do to help?" Johanna asked desperately.

"Why don't you meet me at the St. Charles Hotel tomorrow night? We can plan how to get all of his important papers back," Malcolm pushed.

"All right, but I don't know how to get the cigar box back from those Union soldiers that kidnapped me." Johanna explained.

"We will figure it out. I think you still have something they want. They won't be far behind us," Malcolm announced.

Johanna stared at Malcolm as he sat opposite her. He really was adorable even with a black eye.

"Could you please tell me why you were fighting with that soldier at the Beauregard's?" she asked.

"Oh, that. Did you recognize him?" he asked.

Johanna lied, "no, I did not. Was I supposed to?"

"No. I guess not. He was the one you encountered on the balcony," Malcolm said testing her.

"Please don't tell me you were fighting over me?" she questioned. She tried to forget the conversation she overheard.

"Well, he said some things about you that a lady should never hear," Malcolm lied.

"Oh my, I didn't know. What did he say?" Johanna asked shocked at Malcolm's words.

"Well, if you must know, he asked me if I was paying for my escort and if you were available. He must have thought you were a lady of the evening," Malcolm said trying to upset Johanna.

"Oh. I see." Johanna's heart sank. It seemed like something David would say. What a fool I am to actually believe that he loved me. I should have never given into his kiss, his kisses. His wonderfully heart pounding kisses.

# # #

"This city is the biggest in the South, how can we possibly find her?" Jacob asked.

"Easy. She is a lady. Let's start at the Garden District. Someone has got to know the Lees," said David.

"We don't have contacts with the elite. Do we?" asked Jacob.

"I am going to look for my brother, maybe he will know something," Preston added.

"Good idea, Preston. Jacob and I will split up and ask around, see if anyone knows her whereabouts," said David. "She's got to have some kind of connection from here, friends or relatives."

Chapter 11

"Abigail, it is so nice to see you!" said Johanna as she hugged her friend. "I have missed you so very much."

"Johanna, oh how I have missed you too," Abigail equally excited to see her dearest friend.

"How is married life?" Johanna asked.

"It's pretty amazing, I would have to say," Abigail went on, "although I do miss you coming over for a chat and a cup of tea."

"Me too, thank you for letting me stay with you while I am here," said Johanna as she scanned Abigail's parlor. "I heard New Orleans is a magical place."

Abigail eyed Johanna with curiosity. "Okay Johanna, what is going on with you? You are never one for small talk. What is on your mind?"

"What do you mean?" asked Johanna.

"First of all, I got word from my cousin Mary Alice and she told me all about the ball and your three handsome gentlemen, is this true?" Abigail asked with no reserve in her manner.

"They are not all gentleman," said Johanna thinking of David. "But, they are all very handsome indeed!"

Both of them laughed the way women do when they are together conversing about intimate details.

"Please do tell," said Abigail even more intrigued.

"You are sounding like your cousin now," Johanna grinned and then sighed over her predicament. "Oh Abigail, I have never felt such conflict within my heart. It is silly really, but I don't know what to do?"

"Johanna, this isn't like you," Abigail observed. "You always have been clear on every direction you have taken."

"It seems God has other plans for me," Johanna smiled.

"Yes, sometimes He does. Well, how do you feel about each one of them?" Abigail said trying to help Johanna sort out her feelings. "Let's start with the dashing Rene Beauregard!"

"Oh Abigail really, that is absurd. Rene and I just met and I think he needs someone a little more adventurous than I. It would be hard to keep up with his aristocratic lifestyle. And by the way, could you imagine Clarice being my sister-in-law?" Both women grimaced and then laughed.

"Well, if you change your mind, I just want to let you know that he is in town staying at his family's house," Abigail said with a wink.

"I will keep that in mind when I am desperate for a genuine heartache," teased Johanna.

"Okay, let us move on to your number two man," said Abigail, with a big grin on her face and her curiosity mounting.

"All right, you are truly making me sound like a harlot," laughed Johanna. She continued anyway, "Malcolm is adorable, you should see those dimples when he smiles. It makes your heart melt. He can make me feel important, like I am the only one for him. It truly is a gift I am sure he spent time perfecting."

"You don't trust him?" asked Abigail.

"No, it's not that," said Johanna. "He is a perfect gentleman, handsome, and kind."

"Okay then," said Abigail, eying Johanna. "What's the problem?"

Johanna sighed, "The problem is number three."

# # #

"Did you find her?" asked Jacob.

"Not yet, but I did get in touch with the vixen from Charleston. It seems she is also in town. I think I can use her to my advantage once again," said David smiling.

"Isn't there some kind of riff between her and Miss Lee? Are you sure you want to do that?" Jacob asked with concern.

"They definitely have some history," David agreed. "But they run in the same circles. She is a perfect cover for me to get to Johanna."

"What do you plan on doing once you finally find her?" asked Jacob.

"First and most important making sure she is safe away from Graystone," David said with a determined look on his face.

"Then are you going to whisk her away from her family and take her to Harrisburg? Do I need to remind you about Kathleen? Or are you planning on marrying her too?" asked Jacob trying to get David to think about his actions.

"Don't be so dramatic, Jacob, you are making it sound like a Greek tragedy," David laughed.

"It very well maybe if you don't get killed before this ends," Jacob warned him.

"Killed? Are you insinuating that Malcolm will kill me before he lets me have Johanna?" asked David laughing at the thought.

Jacob ignored David's question. "This is maddening to watch."

"What do you mean my friend?" asked David.

"I have never seen you act like this before, at least about a woman," said Jacob.

"She is not just some woman," said David serious now.

"No, she is not," agreed Jacob. He sighed as he eyed David, "I am concerned about you. Do you really love her or is this some crazy infatuation?"

David bit his lip, contemplating Jacob's question. He sighed and then smiled at his friend, "I really love her."

Chapter 12

*J*ohanna felt the rush of adrenaline as she made her way through the cobblestone streets of Port of New Orleans. The French Quarter was a surprising place to be. The sounds of trombones and saxophones came out of every corner bar, the smell of incense and tobacco filled the streets, and candles flickered highlighting the drunken soldiers and sailors standing on the sidewalks talking to scanty clothed women. She tried not to notice any of this. She was determined to meet Malcolm and begin her trip to

Virginia, to family once again.

Louisiana had just passed the vote and the state had now officially seceded. People were celebrating anyway they knew how. Fireworks filled the evening sky while people cheered at the sight. She couldn't even remember which side she was on or supposed to be on. She thought about David. How long would he be on her side? If Virginia seceded, they would forever be at odds. Right now they were both from the Union. How long would that last, days, weeks, or months? How long did they have?

She wondered how far north she would have to travel to be an ally of his. Why she was thinking of him again in a loving way perplexed her.

The St. Charles Hotel was connected to small shops and apartments. She couldn't quite make out the figures standing overhead looking out balconies and whistling and laughing while she grasped the door of the hotel to enter. She refused to look up and acknowledge their misbehavior. She hesitated and took a deep breath and opened the door.

"Excuse me, I am looking for someone I am supposed to meet here," Johanna asked a hotel attendant who happen to be walking by her as she entered. Johanna was about to describe Malcolm when he grumbled.

"Try over there," he pointed toward a table where a man sat, it appeared the hotel attendant was too busy to be bothered.

The man who he pointed to sat at a small table alone, glasses barely fit on top of his nose. He seemed to be trying to read scraps of paper that lay out in front of him, he was mumbling to himself. Johanna started toward him when a woman with a hooded cloak interrupted her path.

"Please come with me," she ordered Johanna.

No words were spoken between them as they walked silently toward the hotel's cellar steps. A light flickered from below as they descended. Before Johanna reached the bottom stair, a feeling of uneasiness pricked at her, but it was too late to turn back.

"I am looking for Mr. Graystone," she tried to ask the woman whose face was still covered by her cloak. "Have you seen him, Private Malcolm Graystone?"

The woman made no reply until they reached the end of the stairs. Lantern lights flickered in the dark exposing a single door at the end of a hallway.

"The one you seek may not be the one you desire," she smiled pulling her cloak off her head.

Johanna was surprised to see a beautiful young woman with dark features her Creole accent only enhanced her beauty. Johanna watched the woman walk gracefully toward the door and knocked once and then twice more.

The door opened and Johanna was pushed through a darkened room that was only lit by a small candelabrum which sat alone in the center of the room. Johanna focused on its light. Then she noticed the shadowy figure that ominously sat behind it.

"Welcome, Johanna Lee," a rough voice came out of the darkness. Each candle flame swayed with each breath he took. Johanna continued to focus on the candles, their wax melting and slowly cascading down making a shape she could not place.

"Do I know you?" she asked with fear in her voice.

"I don't think so," he laughed. "But you will get to know me soon enough." His men laughed.

"Do you know where I can find Mr. Graystone?" she

asked ignoring his insinuation.

"Yes and no." he came out of the darkness.

Johanna gasped. She knew who he was. He was Captain Darren Myers. But, he wasn't a captain, more like a pirate. He stole cargo ships in harbors and kidnapped women in ports.

"Ah, you recognize me from the wanted posters," he grinned with excitement.

Johanna still speechless stood still.

"They don't do me justice. I think I am much more handsome in person," he laughed. "Don't you think?"

Johanna stepped backwards. The room had now brightened and she now could see Myers' men blocking the stairs to her exit. The lamps they held flickered casting shadows about the room. Johanna noticed the woman who had led her into danger had now vanished.

"What do you want?" she asked with more courage than she actually had.

"You are in possession of something that is very valuable. It will come in handy as a bargaining tool for my freedom," Myers grumbled.

"I have nothing in my possession," she replied.

"Oh but you do, my sweet," he said.

Johanna stared him down, "I am telling you, I have no jewelry or anything of value on me."

Captain Myers laughed and his men followed. Shadows continued to dance around the room, giving it a haunted feeling.

"Jewels and money I have plenty of. That is not what I am speaking of," Myers continued. "Freedom is what I seek."

"There is no way anyone would give you pardon for what you have done. Not even for all the riches in the world," Johanna said in frustration.

"No, but for winning a war, there are those who would sell their souls," Myers said.

"You must be mistaken," she said. "I do not have anything in my possession worth any value." She again surprised herself with her lack of fear.

"Oh, I think you do pretty lady," said Myers. "There is a rumor that your uncle is friends with a balloonist. He made a secret map for him, an original. It is a treasure many men will pay for and even die for, and many women too."

The men in the room laughed. There were more than she first thought.

"I am sorry you must be mistaken. I have nothing, and if I did, I still would not give it to you," she boldly declared.

"Oh, I do like feisty women," Captain Myers laughed. "It's a shame I have to let you go."

"You will let me go?" she asked.

"As soon as I get what I want from you," Myers explained.

"I have nothing, I tell you," Johanna repeated.

"Yes, you said that. Maybe I should have my men search you?" he asked. "I know they would enjoy that immensely."

The men in the room laughed and cheered in agreement.

"You wouldn't?" asked Johanna now frightened.

"Maybe, I will keep you instead for my collection," he stared her down. "I bet I could get a pretty penny for you."

"You can't keep me here," warned Johanna who was

now frightened. "I am in the care of the U.S. Army and they know where I am. If you take me, they will hunt you down like the dog that you are."

"It seems you have forgotten who I am," Myers laughed at her courage. "I have many friends and family that are hidden in the deepest, darkest shadows, Miss Lee."

"I'm not surprised," Johanna said under her breath. "What do you want from me?" she asked.

"I will give you until dawn to retrieve my items," said Myers. "We will find you. Remember any inquiries from the local authorities and you will not live to see another sunrise."

"By dawn, is that a joke? I don't even know if I will ever see him again," Johanna frustrated now being threatened once again. "And besides, that's only a few hours away."

"Then you better hurry," said Myers grinning.

Suddenly to everyone's surprise, a hidden door behind Johanna suddenly slammed open. Johanna, caught in the door's path, was knocked to the ground. With no time to brace herself, she hit her head hard onto the basement floor.

Men she didn't recognize rushed through the secret door, their guns in hand. Myers' men who had been taken by surprise, found themselves surrounded now by a new set of men who had descended the basement steps from behind.

Before everything went black, Johanna saw a figure of a man standing in the doorway.

Johanna teetered in and out of consciousness. She tried desperately to keep her senses. She had now become aware of the extreme ache that pounded the back of her head. Even with her vision blurry, she tried to focus on the men who fought before her. Their confrontation seemed to escalate with angry words but they seemed too far away for her to comprehend what they were saying.

"Your business here has ended," said a voice. "I suggest you leave the premises immediately. The authorities are on their way."

"We don't want any trouble," said Myers raising his hands in defeat. "We will leave."

"She must be quite a handful if you need all these men here," mocked the man.

"Yes, she is quite captivating. Don't you think?" asked Myers.

"Absolutely," he answered.

Captain Myers nodded to his men to halt their brawl and leave. Before he followed, he leaned down near Johanna who still lay motionless on the cold basement floor.

"We will meet again, my lady. That you can count on," he warned Johanna.

Johanna tried to respond, but no words would form on her lips. A dark shadow of a man stood tall over her, but before she could recognize him, darkness enveloped her.

"Bonjour, ma chérie," he said looking down on Johanna. "It seems we meet again."

Chapter 13

"I found her," said Preston, putting his hand on David's shoulder.

"You found her? Where is she?" asked David.

"Well, I know where she was," Preston added.

"And where was she?" David asked feeling like they were finally getting closer.

"She was at the St. Charles Hotel down in the French Quarter, but it seems there was an incident," said Preston.

"An incident, what do you mean by that?" asked David.

"She was introduced to some pirates," Preston smiled. "I guess she was meeting Malcolm there and instead found herself in the hotel's basement being harassed."

"Did they hurt her?" David asked now sick to his stomach.

"Well, yes and no. It seems they were being paid to get information from her. They didn't touch her if that is what you mean," Preston said.

David's fear subsided but was still concerned. "What happened then?" he asked.

"There was a scuffle and she got knocked out. It got hazy from there. No one is sure who actually took her after that," Preston said.

"Someone took her?" David asked now horrified.

"It wasn't the pirates," Preston assured him. "The townspeople refuse to give me any answers. I think they know but wouldn't tell me.

"Then the St. Charles Hotel is where I am going," David said determined to get to the bottom of Johanna's disappearance. "I am going to find someone to give me some answers."

# # #

"Johanna, are you okay? Can I get you anything?"

"Rene, what are you doing here?" Johanna rubbed her aching head.

"I pay a lot of money to keep me posted on everything that happens in my hometown. Nothing gets by me." He handed her a glass of water. "I am sorry you were put in this predicament. You are safe now."

"Where am I?" Johanna just now realized she was not at the St. Charles Hotel any longer.

"Miss Johanna, welcome to the Beauregard House," Rene smiled his most handsome, charming smile.

"I am so confused. How did I get caught up in pirate affairs?" she asked him.

"I have an idea, but we need not think about that right now. Let's just be thankful you are safe," said Rene with a look of concern on his face. "I have let Mrs. Jenkins know you are safe and will be my guest for the night."

"Oh, thank you Mr. Beauregard. I appreciate your kindness," Johanna smiled and winced from the pain in her head simultaneously. "I don't want to be any trouble." Johanna tried to sit up but felt nauseous and had to lie down once again.

"Nonsense, you are no trouble at all," Rene smiled. "Let's get you a cup of tea. We can discuss how you are going to return my kindness in the morning."

Johanna tried to laugh at Rene's insinuation, but she fell asleep instead.

Rene covered up his sleeping guest and leaned in and gently kissed her on the forehead. His eyes traced Johanna's beautiful face and he smiled thinking about how lucky he was to find her and save her once again. He was enjoying his new role saving the damsel in distress. She was what he had been looking for. She was feisty and charming, and what he loved the most, she wasn't going to make it easy for him. Johanna was going to take some real finessing to fall for him. It was a challenge he was willing to take on. He blew out the lamp light before he left the room smiling to himself as he thought of his new conquest.

# # #

"Where is she? What have you done with her?" David grabbed Malcolm by the shirt and slightly lifted him up.

"I don't know. She was supposed to meet me here last night," Malcolm pulled himself away from David. "I got delayed and she never showed up."

"Where is she staying? Have you tried there?" David continued to interrogate Malcolm.

"I did. They said she never showed up last night, her friend is very concerned about her safety." Malcolm said as he straightened his overcoat that David had now let go of.

"If anything has happened to her," David didn't finish his sentence. He glanced at Preston. "Preston, could you go there and wait to see if she shows up."

Preston nodded in agreement and left hastily out the St. Charles Hotel door.

"This seems to be about a lot more than just some military plans to follow her here, should you let me in on the secret?" Malcolm asked David.

David looked at Malcolm with contempt and never answered his question.

"What kind of escort are you? Why did you bring her to New Orleans? You know the Colonel would never step foot here. Unless he wants to leave the Union and that is not happening while Virginia is still part of it." David asked.

"I only follow orders and Lee said to bring her here. What does she have in her possession that you didn't get from her in South Carolina?" asked Malcolm.

David considered telling Malcolm hoping he would just leave her alone once he got the map from her. David knew that Malcolm wouldn't stop especially if he could hurt David in any way.

"This telegram just arrived for you," the hotel attendant handed it to Malcolm.

"Thanks," he read it and then smiled at David. "I guess I will get to her first," Malcolm tipped his hat. "Good day."

As Malcolm left the hotel David turned to Jacob. "Jacob, follow him, I have to find out what happen last night. I need to know if she is safe."

# # #

"What is she doing here?" Clarice asked Rene. "Are we taken in strays now?"

"Miss Lee is here as my guest, and I advise you to keep your voice down, she should be coming in any time now." Rene ignored his sister's question.

"Please tell me you're making jest. You aren't seriously into her? You can do so much better, you have many times." Clarice continued.

"Oh Clarice, don't be vulgar," Rene snapped.

"Do I have to remind you her parents fled to Paris in financial ruin and left her here alone, destitute," Clarice recapped.

"All the more reason she needs friends," Rene defended her.

"Friends, please Rene, you can't be just friends with women. Especially that one! She is a Lee."

"Her uncle is well respected, a West Point graduate," explained Rene.

"And a Union one, she is a traitor! We have a traitor in our home," announced Clarice. "I won't have it. I want her out by morning."

"We only left the union a week ago," said Rene with one raised eyebrow at his sister's ranting. "Clarice you are being emotional. What do you have against her?"

"What do I have against her you say? She ruined all my plans for engagement to the most handsome man I have ever laid eyes upon. He left my party looking for her."

"Such nonsense from you, you couldn't be engaged as much as I," laughed Rene. "We are alike Clarice. There is no one that could entice us enough to only want one lover forever."

"I thought maybe he could be," she laughed, "well at least he could be fun for awhile." They both smiled.

"Well, maybe that is how I feel about Johanna," said Rene. "I am actually having fun trying to win her heart."

"Why do you care to win her heart?" asked Clarice curious now.

"She is mesmerizing. I can't seem to get her out of my mind," confessed Rene.

"Rene, I am not wasting another minute talking about someone who won't matter to you by tomorrow," Clarice ignored his comment. "Listen, my soldier has sent me a telegram and is coming here today, I need her to be out of the house, and I don't want her to distract him from me."

"How could anyone be distracted with you in the room?" asked Rene.

"Well, I am sure she will find a way," said Clarice pouting. "She is a devil that one. She just wants to hurt me."

"She has too much class to worry about you. She is an angel," Rene exclaimed sighing.

"Oh Rene, I hardly thinks so," said Clarice surprised by her brother's new infatuation. "You need to get her out of here. I don't want her here, understood?"

"Okay, I will take her out for the day, but she is staying as my guest for as long as I want," explained Rene.

"Fine, just don't be here when he gets here," said Clarice frowning as she thought about them together and left the room.

Johanna approached Rene missing Clarice all together.

"Good morning, I pray you slept well." Rene said as he sat at the breakfast table holding a chair for Johanna.

"I did, thank you Mr. Beauregard," she smiled.

"Oh, are we using formal names again? I thought we were friends," Rene asked a bit disappointed.

"Do you have any idea how I can get in touch with my uncle?" she ignored his comments.

"Actually I sent a telegram this morning to my father letting him know that you were my guest and to contact Colonel Lee.," replied Rene.

"Oh, thank you, Mr. Beauregard," Johanna said relieved.

"It is my pleasure to serve you," he smiled delighted he could make her happy. "What happened to Malcolm? I thought he was escorting you to Arlington?"

"He was, I was supposed to meet him at the hotel, he never showed up," explained Johanna as she took a bite of her biscuit.

"Well that's no way to treat a lady," Rene said.

"No it's not," Johanna concurred.

"Why were you in the basement of the hotel anyway?" Rene asked.

"I thought Malcolm was down there," said Johanna. "I was led by some woman dressed in a cloak."

"You followed a woman in a cloak to the basement in a hotel?" Rene questioned Johanna's sanity.

"I know. Not a very intelligent decision," she slightly laughed. "I guess I just got caught up in all the cloak and dagger secrecy stuff. My uncle insisted I not trust anyone. I had to learn this lesson the hard way."

"Well, you can trust me," Rene smiled and Johanna returned the smile.

"Now that I am here in New Orleans, I don't know how I am ever going to get to Arlington?" said Johanna.

"Don't worry. We will think of something, even if I have to take you myself." Rene reassured her as he patted her hand. "Meanwhile, let's have some fun today. How about I show you around my city? Have you ever road a street car before?"

Chapter 14

Johanna met Rene in the tea room in the Beauregard's home. His gaze locked onto the garden before him with a troubled look on his face.

"What is it Rene? You seem perplexed," Johanna asked.

Rene looked out into the horizon as he spoke, "Oh, it just that I feel that I am overwhelmed by life's stresses and under whelmed by the joy it gives."

"One must find joy within oneself first to be able to see it anywhere else," Johanna assured him.

Rene smiled. "Yes, I know, you are right." They sat in comfortable silence.

"My sister is here. I apologize for her already. She is in one of her moods again," said Rene.

"No need to worry. I have a lot of practice dealing with your sister and her moods," Johanna smiled.

"You and her have some kind of falling-out between you?" he asked.

"You could definitely say that," Johanna said not wanting to elaborate.

"Well, I hope she doesn't spoil our evening," Rene frowned.

"I hardly believe she could," Johanna tried to reassure him.

"Would you like to tell me what it is?" he asked trying not to pry.

"Why your sister and I don't get a long?" she asked.

"Yes," said Rene curious.

"Oh, I was dear friends with someone long ago who had the unfortunate loss of having to find out her love was secretly courting your sister in New Orleans. It seemed Clarice knew about my dear friend, but my friend did not know about Clarice," Johanna sighed. "She just got empty promises of love and marriage and Clarice got the man."

"Ouch. Well, I am sorry she was caught in the middle of my sister's love affairs. Unfortunately, she doesn't count any man off limits," confessed Rene.

"My friend was devastated at first," Johanna continued. "She was young. She thought she could trust everyone. It was quite humiliating for her. It seemed she was the only one not in the know."

"That is usually how it works," explained Rene.

"Yes. That is true. But, you know, after she stepped away from the situation she realized how thankful she was that she was protected from an awful, loveless marriage. She also finally figured out that happiness doesn't come from someone else," Johanna explained.

"It takes a few heartaches to understand that sometimes," Rene agreed.

"Yes, that is also true," Johanna now surprised at Rene's observation.

"Whatever happened to him?" Rene asked.

"He got what he wanted and got what he deserved," Johanna explained with sadness in her voice.

"He got my sister and good taste of his own medicine," Rene figured out.

"Yep, your sister didn't want him anymore once she got him. Clarice had moved on to someone else," said Johanna.

"Did he ever try to get in touch with your friend, you know, to make amends?" asked Rene.

"He wrote a letter to apologize. But, sometimes we have to realize that God has a better plan for us. Whatever people might do to hurt us, it really doesn't matter. God can make things turn out for our good," Johanna smiled. "She married a fine man who adores her and gave her four beautiful children."

"Well, in your case, you are safe with me. We don't believe in courting family here," Rene laughed.

Johanna laughed right back, "Well, I am glad of that, Mr. Beauregard."

Rene smiled looking on Johanna fondly, "Enough of this serious talk, let us have tea."

# # #

"Mr. Graystone! I thought I would never see you again," smiled Johanna genuinely happy to see him.

"Miss Lee, I am so sorry for the confusion. I hope you are all right." Malcolm approached her and kissed her hand gently. "Please forgive me."

"I will only if you can you explain yourself? Where have you been this whole time?" Johanna asked a little perturbed at Malcolm's absence.

"Trying to find you, I am afraid. I had gotten word that we were to meet your uncle at the boat docks. I sent a telegram to inform you to meet us there, but it must not have made it in time," said Malcolm.

"No I did not receive any message," said Johanna.

"When I went to the hotel I asked around and someone recognized your description, but wouldn't tell me anything," said Malcolm. "Especially that it was Rene who had saved you from an awful situation."

Rene's smile widened.

"It seems the townspeople are all fond of him for some reason," said Malcolm. "They thought I was collecting a debt or something and sent me in the wrong direction a few times."

"I think it is you who now are indebted to me, Malcolm," Rene laughed.

"Shut up, Rene," Malcolm smiled but wouldn't take his eyes off of Johanna.

"All right Mr. Graystone, I will forgive you on one condition," said Johanna.

"And what is that?" he asked returning her smile.

"You take me to Virginia, no more delays," said Johanna.

"You have a deal. I have already secured a steamship for us. We are to leave by morning. And now that I have found you," Malcolm was cut off.

"Thanks to me," Rene chimed in.

"I will never leave your side again," finished Malcolm. His smile now showing his dimple, he put his hand on her cheek.

"Hey, none of that," Rene interrupted.

Johanna faced Rene, "Mr. Beauregard, how can I ever thank you for your hospitality?"

Rene added, "And for saving your life?"

Johanna laughed, "Yes, and for saving my life."

"I don't know I will have to think it over and let you know," Rene joked.

"Okay, sounds good," Johanna smiled.

"I hear you rode a street car for the first time today?" asked Malcolm trying to keep Johanna engaged and eyes off of the handsome Rene Beauregard.

"I did. It was very exciting," said Johanna smiling. "New Orleans is a beautiful city."

"She was so nervous I held her hand the whole time," Rene rubbed it in.

"I am sure you did," Malcolm said with distaste.

"Dinner is now being served," said a servant who interrupted their conversation. "Please follow me."

"I am afraid I can't stay," admitted Malcolm. "I have to secure our departure for the morning." He kissed Johanna's hand once again. "I will send for a carriage to pick you up and take you to the harbor. I will meet you there. You are almost home." Malcolm eyed Johanna.

Johanna pondered the word "home." She had been in so many places in the past month she didn't even remember where home was.

"That's okay Malcolm she will be in good hands," Rene grinned. "I will take good care of her."

Malcolm frowned, "I am sure you will."

"Thank you Mr. Graystone," Johanna ignored Rene's insinuation. "I will see you soon."

"So much for not ever leaving your side," Rene quipped.

"Oh, don't you worry I wouldn't miss our trip for anything." Malcolm looked at Rene. "Besides, on the ship Rene won't be around to interrupt us anymore!"

"Ah, and to my chagrin too," Rene smiled at Johanna.

While Malcolm disappeared out the door, Rene held his arm out to Johanna.

"Are you ready for dinner?" Rene asked.

"Yes. I think I am ready," Johanna smiled up at him.

"I must tell you how absolutely enchanting you look this evening," said Rene in his charming accent.

Johanna blushed. "Thank you, Rene," Johanna used his first name in recognition of their friendship.

Rene smile brightened, "I am getting closer."

"Closer to what pray tell?" Johanna questioned him.

"Closer to you falling in love with me, of course," Rene smiled.

"Not quite yet," she laughed.

"Oh, I forgot to mention," Rene continued as they walked toward the dining hall, "we have a few guests coming. I hope you don't mind."

"What do you mean a few guests?" Johanna questioned him but they had walked into a room full of guests sitting at a large table.

Johanna gasped as she surveyed the guest list. To her utter surprise David was sitting next to Clarice. Clarice's hand was resting on his shoulder. She smiled at Johanna in a protective tiger kind of way.

David smiled up at Clarice not looking at Johanna until he followed Clarice's gaze.

Johanna was surprised that David wasn't shocked by her appearance. He nodded in recognition and then carefully looked back up at Clarice.

"I see, it seems you can't quite keep away from my dear brother," Clarice said with a sly smile.

"Hello Clarice," Johanna looked at her and then once again at David.

"You haven't met my David, have you?" she asked Johanna, smirking. She had sat down and was now leaning into David proudly showing off her new possession.

Johanna hated Clarice for calling David hers. It made her insides hurt. She stared them both down. She felt such conflict, it clouded her judgment. So in a voice that was cold and calculated, she said, "no I have not. Is he one of your new pets?"

Clarice laughed at Johanna's observation. David smiled.

"Miss Lee," Rene interrupted, "did you notice our other guests, Mr. and Mrs. Jenkins?"

Johanna turned toward Abigail. "Oh, it is so nice to see you again," she smiled.

Abigail smiled back with a quick squeeze to her arm. Johanna sat next to her getting the hint.

"Lovely party," Abigail said, "Don't you think?"

"It's lovely all right," Johanna frowned looking once again at David.

He was lost in conversation with Clarice. She tried not to study his new clean shaven face that only enhanced his good looks. She tried only to focus on her anger toward him for being involved once again with Clarice.

Clarice was enjoying Johanna's glances and played up to them. With every once in awhile caressing his cheek, whispering in his ear closely, and laughing at everything he would say.

Johanna watched what looked like an intimate conversation between David and Clarice. It was like a knife that continued to stab her over and over every time Clarice touched him.

"I am so glad you are here," Abigail said to Johanna trying to distract her.

"It was so nice of Rene to invite you and your husband, John," said Johanna realizing her error in letting David's affection toward Clarice bother her.

Johanna than turned to Rene, "Thank you so much for such a lovely day."

"Did you enjoy yourself, Miss Lee," Rene asked smiling.

"I did very much," she smiled back at him.

She felt David's gaze upon her, but she refused to look in his direction.

"You should see what I am planning for us tomorrow?" said Rene.

"I truly look forward to it," said Johanna.

"Johanna," Abigail whispered to her, "so what is this I hear you are staying here instead of with me?"

"What do you mean?" asked Johanna.

"I received a telegram from Mr. Beauregard telling me you had a change of plans and that you will be staying here with him as his guest for the duration of your stay," said Abigail.

"He said that in his telegram? That sounds like something he would do," Johanna smiled as she looked at Rene who was now engaged in a conversation with Abigail's husband, John.

"Is it true?" asked Abigail, confused by her friend's reaction. "Are you staying here with Rene?"

"Well, I know he assumes that every woman wants to be with him, but it sounds intriguing doesn't it, Abigail?" asked Johanna who was not that shocked at Rene's forwardness.

"Johanna! I am surprised at you," said Abigail laughing as quietly as she could. "Are you starting to fall for your number one?"

"Oh, Rene is wonderful, but it is extremely distracting when number three is here," Johanna motioned toward David who was now leaning into Clarice for an intimate whisper.

"You are kidding me, he is Mr. McPherson?" asked Abigail intrigued. "You mean the man with Clarice at his side?"

"Unfortunately, yes," Johanna sighed.

Clarice must have heard her name and looked up across the table staring at Johanna.

She smiled and said, "I guess you will be leaving soon. Just as well, there is nothing left for you here." She stared Johanna down and then gently put her hand on David's with a grin. "Rene has to return to papa in Charleston."

Johanna ignored Clarice's jab and looked at Rene with disappointment.

"Is this true?" she asked.

"Yes, I am afraid it is," Rene answered her with a little regret in his voice.

"I am sorry to hear this. You will truly be missed," Johanna smiled at him.

"I knew I would get to you sooner or later Miss Lee," Rene smiled.

Johanna blushed but smiled anyway. She glanced at David who had not seemed to look her way throughout most of dinner, was now eyeing her with curiosity.

"My brother," said Clarice looking at everyone around the room for a dramatic effect, "you have truly outdone yourself this evening."

"What do you mean Clarice?" asked Rene not sure where she was going with the conversation.

"You usually wait until the holidays to help out those less fortunate than us," Clarice smiled.

No one knew how to respond to her insult except Rene.

"Clarice, my humble sister, have you not so told me yourself that charity begins at home?" asked Rene.

"I did?" she asked.

"Well, then you are correct to assume that I have been charitable to you. You are very fortunate to be in Miss Lee's presence this evening. Her family is on the path to greatness. Being friends with her will only increase our position," Rene smiled.

Clarice stared at Rene. She wasn't used to being put in her place. She didn't like it one bit.

It killed David that he couldn't protect Johanna from Clarice's stings. He needed to continue his charade until Johanna was safely out of the Beauregard's house, away from Malcolm and with her family in Arlington.

Finding Clarice here was a mixed blessing. She got him in the door so he could get to Johanna, but he also had to deal with Clarice and her strong personality.

Clarice wasn't done with Johanna. Not by a long shot.

"Johanna, you definitely can tell you are not from here," Clarice eyed Johanna.

"And why is that?" Johanna asked waiting for the sting.

"You don't seem to really care about your appearance like most New Orleans' ladies," Clarice continued. "After all, how old is that gown you are wearing?"

Rene tried to intervene but Johanna got to her first.

"Oh, yes, I would have to agree with you, my dress doesn't seem to come off as easily as yours when a handsome man is near," Johanna clammed back.

The room went into a frizzy. Clarice sat in silent shock at Johanna's comeback, while David coughed into his drink. John, Abigail's husband, laughed out loud without any discretion, and Abigail scolded her friend in a loud whisper, "Johanna."

Rene stood up quickly, "Okay, anyone up for a game of cards?"

Chapter 15

After Clarice and Johanna's confrontation everyone moved into the parlor. They all tried pretending there wasn't tension floating through the room. They each felt uncomfortable for very different reasons.

Rene and John migrated toward the card table and the women to the sitting chairs. David did neither. Instead he went toward the piano and asked Clarice if she minded he played.

"Be my guest," Clarice smiled. She seemed to not be able to take her eyes and hands off of his handsome face. Johanna thought he winced when Clarice touched his cheek softly, but she figured it was only wishful thinking.

"That was some scene at dinner," Abigail said to Johanna.

"I don't know where she gets off thinking she can talk to people that way," said Johanna.

Abigail and Johanna watched Clarice stand near David who was now playing New Orleans on the piano.

"Apparently he came all the way here for a visit," explained Johanna.

"For her or for you?" questioned Abigail.

"Oh I love this piece by Bach," Clarice seemed to intensify her voice so others were aware of her being well educated in music.

"It's Jesu, Man's Desire, isn't it?" announced Rene laughing at the women's reaction to his observation.

"He is sure putting on a show isn't he?" said Johanna speaking of David.

"All men do in front of Clarice," Abigail confirmed. "At least my John is not tempted by the temptress."

"Yes, you are truly blessed my friend," Johanna tried to smile.

"Johanna, what are you going to do now?" asked Abigail.

"I am going to Arlington," she said. "There is nothing for me here. Besides, I think I have worn out my welcome."

"You think so?" Abigail laughed.

Johanna smiled and then continued to watch David. She tried not to but she could literally feel his presence envelope her. She hated that. Her face flushed thinking of his kiss once again. She just hoped it wasn't apparent to everyone else.

"Are you going to be okay," Abigail asked concerned about Johanna.

"I will be fine," Johanna said convinced. "Besides, I have number one and two to fall back on."

"Well, Rene seems smitten with you. That is amazing in itself," Abigail said.

"I don't think it's that amazing. You just have to act like you're not interested and he is near panting like a dog," Johanna laughed.

"Johanna, that is terrible," said Abigail as she tried to suppress her laugh. "I don't know what men see in Clarice," said Abigail as she too was watching the scene unfold in front of her.

"Oh, your right, she is just beautiful, charming and seductive. Nothing impressive," smiled Johanna.

They continued to watch the two together. It was hard for her to have David so close in proximity without being near him. She felt the heaviness of disappointment begin to pull her down. She really believed he once had strong feelings for her. It still hurt when she thought of the conversation she overheard between Malcolm and David. He denounced any feelings he had for her, saying that it was all for some mission. She was played a fool and now he sat at Clarice's side. It felt like déjà vu. This time she had to watch it play out in front of her. She received another stab to the heart when Clarice put her hand on his arm and another when she whispered in his ear with a small kiss before she left the room.

David waited until Clarice was completely out of the room and changed the music.

"I know this one, this is My Cottage Home," Rene announced out loud.

Johanna's heart skipped a beat. She thought of her family's cottage with David. She thought of them in the pouring rain, she thought of their passionate first kiss.

David began playing a new tune.

"Oh this is Rainy Day," said Abigail playing the game now.

Johanna looked up at David who was now eyeing her. Her face flushed. He grinned at her. She was taken in by it. She moved toward him cautious but knowing in her heart he had been thinking of that night too.

"I didn't know you played," she whispered.

"You don't know a lot about me, Miss Lee," David continued to play.

"I guess I don't." she confessed.

"My mother taught me. It's not my passion though," he explained.

"What is your passion Lieutenant McPherson?" Johanna asked in a whisper.

"Are you talking to me about passion Miss Lee?" David asked as he gazed at her intently.

She shot right out of her dreamlike state, "No, No I am not," she swallowed nervously and looked around the room. It seemed as if time had stood still. This moment was made for her and David. Their conversation and presence seemed to be unnoticed.

David smiled at her uncomfortable reaction. "You are here with Malcolm or Rene?" he asked.

"Why do you care? It seems you can't keep away from Clarice," said Johanna frustrated.

"I can't keep away from you," he admitted. He then looked up at her and stopped playing.

Johanna's heart skipped. She searched his face to see if he was telling the truth. She loved that handsome face and those sapphire eyes that bore into her soul.

"How could I ever believe you?" she asked in a whisper as she searched his face.

David began to play again. "Where is your dear Mr. Graystone?" he asked.

"I don't know. He seems to keep disappearing on me," explained Johanna. "Why, would you and Malcolm like to entertain the Beauregard family again?"

David ignored her comment. "Do you know anything about Rene Beauregard?" he asked.

"Rene saved me from an awful situation," she added, "rather like what Mr. Graystone did at my family's cottage."

"Yes, when you left me for dead," David came back.

Johanna rolled her eyes, "Where's Clarice anyway? She seems a bit taken in by your charm; she won't stop touching you."

"It's the cost I have to pay to get what I want," David grinned.

"Oh you poor thing, Clarice kissing on you, it's a terrible burden is it? You are meant for each other. Both of you do whatever it takes to get what you want including deceiving someone you pretend to care about," she said biting her lip.

"I am not pretending with you," he said. "I am here because of you."

"You came here for the map," she said frustrated by his attempt to win her over. "Don't tell me otherwise, I overheard you talking about me to Malcolm at the ball."

David's mind flashed back to his conversation with Malcolm. "Why would I ever tell Malcolm how I feel about you?" he asked. "I don't think you realize the danger you truly are in," he whispered to her.

"I am only in danger when you are around," she said with a double meaning.

"That's not what I hear," David said.

Johanna had no comeback. She stared at him in silence.

"Listen, I need that map," said David, "and I need you to stay away from Malcolm."

"You want me to stay away from Mr. Graystone?" she asked. "Why?"

"I have the cigar box and am willing to give it back to you," he said.

"If I give you the map?" she asked him.

"Yes," he answered.

"And you will stop harassing me?" she asked him.

"If that is what you want," he said not looking at her.

Johanna bit her lip. She couldn't answer his question. She had no idea what she desired anymore. She was sure she didn't want him out of her life and she was sure she did.

"But you must promise me you will stay away from Malcolm," David added.

"Why?" she asked again.

"Mr. McPherson," Rene interrupted, "could you please play something I could dance to with my darling Miss Lee?"

Rene grabbed Johanna around the waist and pulled her close. Johanna smiled at her predicament. She wondered if Rene's attention bothered David.

David watched Rene and Johanna dance closely. He fumed with jealousy but continued to play. Clarice entered the room and saw David watching Johanna and Rene intently.

"I don't know what my brother sees in her," she said as she sat next to him on the piano bench.

"Where have you been?" David asked not really caring but intent on keeping up his charade.

"Did you miss me?" she asked not answering him.

"Of course, no room is quite the same without you in it," he said really meaning it.

Clarice's face brightened at his words. She leaned into him whispering, "Why don't you stop playing and spend some time with me?"

"Unfortunately, I must retire for the evening," he said as he looked past her toward Johanna who was smiling now at Rene as he held her close.

"Maybe tomorrow you can call on me?" she asked.

"Absolutely," he said kissing her hand gently.

"Let me walk you to the door," she smiled as she took his hand in hers.

"Thank you, I would like that," he lied.

Johanna was still dancing with Rene when the music abruptly stopped. She and Rene's attention went toward David kissing Clarice's hand and them walking out hand in hand.

Johanna's face went pale. Rene then grabbed her hand and pulled her close to him so they were face to face.

"You are my Archilles' heel, you know that, Johanna? I am enjoying your company more than I would like to admit," he smiled and then kissed her on the cheek.

Johanna smiled at Rene's words and then looked at Abigail who was in awe of Johanna's circumstance, her eyes getting bigger every second.

"I will be right back, I have something for you," Rene said and then walked away.

Johanna walked over to Abigail who was sitting on the couch next to her husband. Abigail mesmerized by Rene's affection toward Johanna.

"Oh stop it, Abigail. He has won you over, but not me, this is part of his little game with women," Johanna insisted.

"It's a great game from where I am sitting," Abigail laughed.

"I must speak with Mr. McPherson before he goes. I just don't know how I am going to get him away from Clarice," Johanna frowned and then exited the room.

Abigail looked at her husband, "I don't know how anyone could get their man away from Clarice."

# # #

When Johanna went toward the drawing room she was cut off by Clarice.

"I just don't get him. He never goes for women beneath him," Clarice stared Johanna down.

"Whom are you speaking of?" Johanna confused by her words.

"Rene of course, charity I would say was never his strong suit. He must have felt desperate this evening. His standards in women have taken quite a dive," Clarice said trying to insult Johanna as much as she could.

"How dare you," Johanna held her ground. "Is this about Rene or are you upset over Mr. McPherson?"

"How do you know him?" Clarice demanded an answer.

"I know that he is not who he portrays," Johanna announced.

"You are so naïve, still after all these years, you still underestimate me," Clarice grinned.

"I know that you can never be trusted, especially when it comes to men," explained Johanna now irritated.

"Are you still harboring resentment towards me for your lost love?" asked Clarice.

"No Clarice. I have made my peace with that a long time ago. You can't help if you are so insecure that you can't find love without stealing someone else's," said Johanna as she stared her down.

"I can't steal anything that doesn't want to be stolen," she laughed. "He pursued me. They all pursue me."

"You seem to make yourself available to all, but never to one, why is that?" Johanna asked. "Is it because you know deep down if the men stayed around long enough they would know how awful you really are?"

Johanna didn't wait for an answer and headed back into the parlor.

"We are leaving," Abigail said as she gave Johanna a hug.

"I am sorry to hear that," said Johanna.

"Did you find him?" whispered Abigail.

"No, I did run into Clarice once again," Johanna smiled.

"Lovely," Abigail smiled back.

"Where is everyone off to?" Rene asked walking into the room with a wrapped gift.

"Thank you for a very entertaining evening," said John as he shook Rene's hand and smiled big toward Johanna.

"I am glad you enjoyed yourself," Rene laughed understanding.

John and Abigail left leaving Johanna alone once again with Rene.

"What do you have there?" Johanna asked Rene who was still holding the gift.

"For you," he said handing it to her. "It's a small reminder of our time together here."

Johanna opened an intricate glass globe inside sat the city of New Orleans covered in snow. "Thank you, this is beautiful," she smiled up at him.

Rene leaned in and kissed her gently on the cheek. "I am glad you like it," he smiled back.

Johanna went to her room holding the snow globe watching the flakes fall on the city. When she entered she noticed it was not as she had left it. On her bed lay her uncle's cigar box. She looked around the room and saw nothing had been taken or disturbed. What was David's motivation for giving her the cigar box before getting the map? Was he really that desperate for her to stay away from Malcolm? Now she was more curious than before. What was it about Malcolm that David despised? He was a good and loyal soldier and a fine gentleman, wasn't he?

Chapter 16

"*I* don't know why you gave her that cigar box back anyway," said Jacob. "We never really figured that out, except that Preston likes them."

"She made a deal with me," said David. "I think if you give me more time I can find out all we want to know."

"Why do you think this?" asked Jacob.

"I think I am softening her up," said David.

"I think Miss Lee is more cunning than we have given her credit for," said Jacob.

"Yes, that is true," David agreed.

"I don't know. How do we know she will tell us? She is a stubborn one," said Jacob.

David smiled at Jacob's observation. "Let's keep an eye on her," said David. "We just might get everything we have been hoping for."

# # #

The woman showed up again. Her dark features enhanced her beauty, which made her appear a lot younger then her age. She had a kind but determined look on her face. When she spoke her Creole accent appeared.

"You have many allies, Johanna Lee. Where does your loyalty lie?" she asked.

"Who are you?" Johanna asked intrigued.

"I am just another spider in your web of deceit," explained the woman cryptically.

Johanna was shocked at the woman's accusation, "I am not deceiving anyone."

"Only yourself," she said.

Johanna felt as if she was speaking in riddles. "Can I help you?"

The woman laughed. "No Miss Johanna, I think it is I who can help you."

"I recognize you. You were the one who delivered me into the hands of the pirate," Johanna realized the woman seemed a lot younger at the hotel. "At least it looked like you."

She laughed again. "You have something in your possession that many would kill for."

"What you are talking about, I don't have with me any longer. I should not be in danger now," Johanna lied.

"I am not talking about any map," said the woman.

"You are being very mysterious. What are you speaking of then?" asked Johanna.

"Your heart," she said.

"I don't know what kind of voodoo you're into, but it's not for sale," Johanna began to walk away.

The woman laughed again. "In my age I know that everything has a price. And your heart will cost you and others plenty."

Johanna frightened now of her words turned back to the woman. "I am sorry, I don't believe in fortune telling."

The woman smiled. "You are taking a very dangerous journey. It can lead to great sadness," she handed Johanna three stones.

Johanna bit her lip. She did not want to encourage the strange woman but she felt she needed to hear her words for some reason.

"One smooth, one rough, and one treasure to behold," the woman said cryptically. "Only your heart will tell you the difference," the woman handed her three rocks. Johanna surprised by the gifts placed them in her handbag.

"Thank you. I will consider your message but I must leave now," Johanna desperately trying to get away.

"Shall I call Rene to come for you?" asked the woman.

"You know Rene? I should have guessed. No thanks. I must be meeting someone at the dock. You can relay a message to him. Tell him I said 'nice try'." Johanna began to walk away. "Oh, I didn't get your name?"

"I don't think you are going anywhere my dear. How's that fever of yours doing?" asked the woman.

Just then Johanna felt a cold breeze pass right through her and with it came an eerie wave of nausea. Before Johanna slipped out of consciousnesses she heard the woman say, "My name is Marie, Marie Laveau."

# # #

Johanna awoke to the handsome face of Rene once more. Before he could speak she bolted upright and yelled, "The Voodoo Queen, Rene? You stopped me from leaving with help from New Orleans infamous Voodoo Queen?"

"Oh Johanna. Don't be so dramatic," Rene grinned. "She is just a friend. The locals call her that. I just call her Marie. She used to be my Mother's hairdresser." Rene smiled at Johanna's anger.   "You don't seem to be running a fever now," He gently caressed her cheek, "I was worried about you."

Johanna brushed him off. "Rene what about the pirate at the St. Charles Hotel, was that you too?"

"Absolutely not, I saved you remember?" he looked

longingly toward her. Johanna couldn't help looking into his handsome face and feeling that he was telling the truth. He softly caressed her hand. She wanted to be angry with him but she just couldn't. She suddenly had this strange feeling of wanting to kiss him, so she quickly diverted her eyes from him before he noticed.

"I only remember the woman in the cloak who looked like your voodoo queen, only younger," said Johanna.

"It was her daughter, also named Marie. I had nothing to do with it. I think it was all a set up by," he trailed off, "someone from the union."

Johanna thought of David again but quickly pushed it aside before it became too vivid.

"Here is some tea. Please drink it, it will make you feel better," he handed her the warm cup. "My sister has left. Please consider staying awhile longer."

"Are you holding me prisoner, Mr. Beauregard?" asked Johanna with a half smile.

"If it will keep you here with me, then yes," and he leaned in and kissed her square on the mouth. He left the room before she could protest or throw the teacup at him whichever was coming first.

Instead Johanna sat in shocked silence. Surprised at what an amazing kiss it really was. She smiled to herself with almost a laugh. She realized how much practice he must have had to perfect his kisses. She put her hand up to her lips feeling the heat from Rene's kiss. It affected her more than she wanted to admit.

"No. No. No." she tried to convince herself shaking her head. Things didn't seem to be getting an easier for her.

Chapter 17

"*I* thought you were meeting me at the dock? Are you still not feeling well?" Malcolm asked with concern in his voice.

"I am fine Malcolm," she patted his arm, "I don't think even a fever will keep me from getting to Virginia," she smiled.

Rene walked in the room with a tray full of cookies and tea. Johanna tried not to look at him, but her eyes were drawn to his handsome face again. Her face warmed thinking of their kiss. He gave her a big smile. No words were spoken between them but Malcolm felt as he had just interrupted something.

"Johanna? Did you hear me?" Malcolm asked.

Johanna feeling more embarrassed she didn't hear what Malcolm said turned to him quickly, "Yes, Mr. Graystone?" she tried to cover.

Rene softly laughed behind them fully aware of his new effect on Johanna.

Malcolm turned around and faced Rene. "Should I be concerned with the time you have been spending with Miss Lee?"

Rene stared at Johanna with longing while he answered Malcolm. A technique he had perfected. "Absolutely," he said smiling.

"Oh Rene, knock it off." Johanna laughed and then said to Malcolm," Rene has been a wonderful friend, but I am ready to go home." Johanna decided she was not going to be tripped off her course for a silly kiss from a man whose joy was the passion of women, especially those who seemed impossible to get. It was a great kiss. But it was not the kiss. He wasn't him and he could never be.

Rene actually looked hurt, but he recovered quickly. "I think she needs to rest." he felt her head. "It seems her fever has returned. I will call the doctor right away." Rene left the room.

Malcolm was silent as he walked towards Johanna and caressed her hand.

"The ship is set to sell tomorrow evening. Do you think you will be ready to leave by then? Malcolm asked her.

"I just need to get rest," Johanna yawned. "I will be ready." Johanna closed her eyes. The fever made her feel suddenly sleepy.

"The doctor is on the way," Rene walked in.

"Didn't you have an epidemic here a few years ago? I hope she has not contracted it," Malcolm said concerned.

"Yes, it was yellow fever, wiped out about 5000 residents two years ago," Rene smiled. "I don't think this is yellow fever. It should wear off soon enough."

"What does that mean?" Malcolm asked not trusting Rene.

"I mean she should feel better soon," said Rene covering his tracks.

"She is asleep now," said Malcolm. "I think we need to get one thing straight."

"And what is that Malcolm?" Rene smiled knowing what was coming.

"She is more important to me than you think," Malcolm announced.

"Guess what Malcolm, I care for her too," Rene smiled.

"Don't say you love her, than I know you are surely jesting," Malcolm laughed.

"It might be dear friend. It just might be," Rene announced to Malcolm and himself.

"Well, I won't stand in your way if she wants you, but I doubt that very much," Malcolm smirked.

"And why is that?" Rene asked.

"Because she is going to marry me on the ship to Virginia, I plan to have the Captain perform the ceremony," Malcolm said confidently.

"Well, won't you be disappointed when she says no."

Rene jabbed, "unless of course you force her, which I wouldn't put past you."

"No need for that. She is falling for me already," Malcolm announced.

"Then why did she kiss me?" smirked Rene.

"Sir," they were interrupted by the housemaid. "The doctor is here."

# # #

"Are you sure you want to leave?" Rene asked Johanna.

"I am sure. It is time for me to go." She smiled at him as he held her hands.

"If I ask you to marry me, would you stay then?" Rene asked actually surprised by his own words.

"Oh Rene," Johanna smiled, "you have been the best part of New Orleans. I will always cherish our time together. I thank you for your hospitality."

"But the answer is no," he answered for her.

'You don't mean it," Johanna smiled.

"But I think I love you," he kept blurting things out desperately. He really didn't want her to go.

"Today you think you do, wait until you meet your next conquest tomorrow," she laughed. She kissed him on the cheek.

Rene frowned, "The coach is waiting for you outside to meet Malcolm at the dock."

"Thank you," Johanna said.

"I would be weary of him," warned Rene. "There is a lot you don't know about him."

"I will," Johanna smiled, thinking he was being a bit jealous.

She walked to the coach and did a small wave goodbye before stepping in. It wasn't enough for him. He ran to her and kissed her passionately. And this time she let go of her pride and let him.

Chapter 18

As they approached a young deckhand Malcolm took her by the hand, "She's my fiancée, soon to be Mrs. Graystone."

Johanna's face warmed, embarrassed by the lie.

Malcolm leaned into her and whispered, "I am sorry, I probably should have discussed it with you first."

"You just caught me off guard that was all," Johanna tried to brush it off.

"Well Miss Johanna," Malcolm bowed, "I would be

honored to have your hand. Then we wouldn't be living a lie and I could give you a home, a family, my love."

Johanna found herself speechless for a moment. How could she have two offers of marriage within an hour of each other? It was mind boggling to her.

"I did not know you felt this way," she said.

"You didn't?" asked Malcolm. "Surprising as it may seem but I have loved you even before we met. Your uncle has talked about you with such joy. I knew I had to meet the woman 'who lights up a room and warms every heart'. And when I saw your family portrait and there you were as beautiful as ever, I believed that there was no other woman for me." He kissed her hand gently.

It was hard for her to take this all in. It wasn't everyday she was proposed to, well, actually today it was. She smirked at the thought of it.

"You haven't answered me. Will you give me the utmost pleasure in accepting my proposal of marriage?" asked Malcolm.

"This has happened so quickly. I feel my head spinning. Will you give me a few days to consider your offer?" she asked with a slight smile.

He smiled back at her, his dimples showing. He was very adorable and she thought at least he didn't try to kiss her. If one more man kissed her without asking she would have to agree with David, she was a Southern whore.

"Of course, but not another moment longer," Malcolm smiled.

"Agreed," she smiled back.

"Let's go prepare ourselves for dinner with the captain," said Malcolm. They walked arm and arm toward their quarters.

A short time later Johanna heard a knock at her cabin door. "Are you ready Mr. Graystone?" she asked.

"I am sorry I won't be joining you," Malcolm said frowning. She looked at him with raised eyebrows. "I've received an urgent telegram. I must leave immediately," said Malcolm.

"Are you not traveling with me?" asked Johanna.

"I will be back before your departure," Malcolm assured her. "My contact doesn't like to be kept waiting. I will catch up with you before you set sail." He looked at the disappointment in her face. "I promise I won't leave you for very long," Malcolm explained mysteriously.

"You've said that before. I do not feel comfortable being alone. Is it safe here?" Johanna looked around the dirty ship with disgust. To her it seemed more like a fishing vessel than a merchant ship.

He caressed her cheek and smiled, "I am sorry. I'll make it up to you. How about I will let you beat me at a game of chess."

"All right, but I can beat you on my own," she smiled back. Johanna was taken in by his handsome smile. It could easily make any girl melt. She hesitated but said anyway, "Don't smile like that for anyone else lest I fear you won't return."

"You are the only one for me." His smile widened and he leaned in and kissed her gently on the cheek.

"Just go. I will see you soon. I will be waiting for you in my cabin." She pushed him away before she was kissed again. He raised his eyebrows at her words. "You know what I mean."

He grinned, "Just stay in your cabin, no one will

bother you. The captain has strict orders to keep my precious cargo safe," said Malcolm.

"Your precious cargo?" questioned Johanna.

He smiled again and disappeared into the fog.

"Well that was mysterious," Johanna said to herself as she walked towards her cabin and locked the door behind her.

The ship's captain shouted orders to pull up the gang plank for the night. His crew eagerly answered his call. Johanna never dreamed she would be a guest on a merchant steamer. This was a new experience for her. She thought about how it had been a lot of new experiences recently for her. She felt the jerk of the ship pulling away from the dock and her heart skipped a beat. Johanna thought how odd that the boat would pull away from the dock over night. She stood to inquire when she knocked over her handbag and the rocks Marie had given her had spilled out onto the floor. She picked them up one by one and studied them. Their texture was similar to Marie's words.

Johanna caressed them and whispered, "One smooth and

one rough." she held them in her hands. It seemed one was

smooth and the other two were rough. She then felt the

small crack the one had in the middle of it. With her thumb

she separated it. To her surprise inside were sparkling

gems, "and one a treasure to behold. Okay. What does this

mean?" she asked herself.

# # #

Johanna stepped out of her room into a glorious

display of colors over the horizon. Her eyes fixed on the

crimson sunset. She marveled at its beauty.

"A beautiful sight, isn't? It doesn't matter how long I

have been out here, I still am awed by God's splendor."

Johanna surprised by the captain's appearance,

smiled. She noticed his uniform was impeccable and he

wore it well. His tanned skin was apparently aged by the

salted sea air and sun. She figured he looked older than his

years.

"It is lovely," she agreed.

"I take it you are going in uncharted territory?" he asked.

"You could say that," Johanna smiled. "I feel like I am on a new adventure, anything is possible." The cool sea air seemed to give her a new sense of freedom and courage.

"I am glad to hear that. I am Captain Thomas O'Reilly. Everyone just calls me Reilly. You are Miss Lee?"

"Yes," Johanna answered. "Could you tell me why we pulled away from the dock? We aren't leaving yet are we?"

"Oh heavens no, it is for our safety. You never know when you could be boarded by pirates. It makes it harder for them to board the ship," he said.

"Pirates, I thought it was safe here in the harbor." She questioned thinking about her ordeal earlier in the week.

"It's just a precaution. I have never been boarded by pirates and I hoped to never." He tried to reassure her.

"Oh. I see, Mal…Mr. Graystone should be back within the hour. At least that is what he said," trying to make herself feel better.

Captain Reilly put his hand on her shoulder. "Don't worry we won't leave until your betrothed arrives."

Johanna slightly embarrassed again by the lie just smiled.

"May I ask why you are here in New Orleans?" he asked.

"It's quite a long story. One I don't really like to talk about," she replied.

"I see. Love is a crazy thing, don't you think? You never can believe what you're capable of until you're faced with heartache," said Reilly.

"Pardon me?" Johanna extremely confused by his words.

"You have a very famous uncle in the Union army. What will he do if Virginia decides to secede? Fight against his family? His friends?" he asked.

"Why does everyone believe that a conflict will arise?" she asked and then continued, "I am not sure. I haven't really thought of it.

"Well, what would you do?" he asked.

"I guess wherever my family goes I will go," she answered shrugging her shoulders slightly.

"Sometimes we have to make hard decisions. Only

God knows what is best for us. Anyway, I have a telegram for you," Captain Reilly handed it to her.

"For me?" asked Johanna surprised.

She took the envelope and watched Reilly walk away. Johanna noticed a deckhand near her who seemed to look familiar, but she couldn't place him. Her fingers trembled as she opened it the parcel. She held her breath;

You're in great danger.
All shall reveal itself in dew time.

Johanna looked around, slightly confused and slightly scared. Dew time? Whoever sent this could not spell. She looked back at the sunset it had changed to a menacing blood red. She went back into her cabin and locked the door behind her.

Johanna did not sleep well. She continued to have disturbing dreams filled with telegrams written in blood and an evil man chasing her into dark alleys all which ended before his hands were upon her, each time waking in sweat only to close her eyes again to began down another dark dead end alley. The last dream she realized her pursuer had no hands and a hooded cloak that shaded his face, she had awakened only by a disturbance outside her cabin. With sweat already on her brow and a heart that beat madly in her chest she quietly got out of her bed and tiptoed toward the door. She listened intently. All seemed quiet except a shuffling down the hall that seemed to be getting further from her. She held her breath a little longer and than relaxed.

"Must have been my imagination," she headed for the bed and quickly decided against trying to enter into another bad dream. She didn't need to be scared any more than she was. The sun had not awakened yet but she was ready for the day. She grabbed her locket and hid it again around her neck under her dress. She decided to explore the ship while everyone was asleep and when her hand grabbed the door handle she noticed it seemed wet.

She quickly lifted her hand a bit disturbed by it, "dew?" The note ran through her mind, 'all will reveal itself in dew time.' Johanna brushed it off and continued out her door. It was still dark, "maybe this is a bad idea," she said to herself under her breath.

Johanna heard the shuffling again to her right and began to follow the noise down the ship's deck. The noise careened around the bow and then halted. She was about to question her sanity, when she stumbled over something in the dark and grabbed the railing for support. It was wet again, but this time it felt sticky. She could barely see her feet or her hands in the thick darkness.

She tried to look at her hand and held it up in the fading moonlight. Johanna jumped from the fear of her realization that blood was on her hand and she fell over coming face to face with one of the young deckhand's dead staring eyes. Johanna tried to scream, but nothing came out. She headed toward her cabin not knowing where to go. She opened it and found it was ransacked, her trunk was emptied and its contents spilled on the floor.

She was glad she was still wearing her mother's locket. Johanna exited her cabin without thinking and headed to Captain Reilly's room. A light shown below his door and it stood slightly ajar. Johanna pushed the door open and stepped in. She was horrified to see Captain Reilly gagged and bound in the corner of his room. The Captain was dead. Johanna whipped around to exit as quickly as possible not knowing if she should hide or try to escape the steamer.

The sun refused to rise and the sea air was cold, dark and unforgiving. She stood still it felt to her like an eternity. She couldn't make her mind up what to do, she couldn't swim and David wasn't around to save her if she tried. She felt like fainting, but Rene was also nowhere to be found. She had no hope in surviving the morning. Fear had taken a hold of her and she was melted to the floor.

"Make a decision," she said to herself, "or you are going to die." So she pushed out of her mind the thought of a killer being aboard and probably searching for her and she continued down the dark hallway. She thought if she made it to a dinghy maybe she could row herself back to shore, it wasn't that far away. Just then two beefy hands grabbed her from behind. She struggled but she was no match for him. He picked her up as if she was a child and he dragged her to the bridge.

"I knew we would meet again Miss Lee," Captain

Myers smiled at her.

"You…you killed the captain," was the only thing Johanna could blurt out.

"I commandeered the ship, I am its captain now," Myers explained. "I now own everything aboard including you."

Johanna couldn't believe this was happening again. She was being kidnapped except this time her captors were vile murderers. This was not turning out to be her year. Johanna searched the room for a way out or a weapon, but it was all in vain. She realized now why she recognized the deckhand. He was one of Myers' men. Johanna felt defeated. No one was going to save her now. They were going to kill her and maybe ravage her first.

"Sit,' said Myers. Johanna obeyed. "Give me your locket." Johanna reluctantly handed it to him.

"I should have known you would hide it on you. Maybe I should have let my men search your body." He smirked while he opened it in triumph.

He unfolded the letter carefully. His eyebrows rose with his confusion. "It seems I was not the only one deceived," said Captain Myers and then handed her the note.

Johanna read it carefully. It took her a few times to understand its meaning. When it did become clear, she knew exactly who it was from.

"Like a thief in the night;
It wasn't just your heart in plight."

Johanna dropped the paper out of her hands and as it fell so did a tear down her soft cheek.

"Ah, you trusted someone you should not have." Myers motioned his men to leave.

"It was stolen from me," Johanna whispered. She looked up at Myers sadly. She was surprised to see that he actually seemed to have felt sorry for her.

"Now you know why I became a pirate. I too was deceived by someone I loved," said Myers. "Here this will make you feel better," he handed her a mug.

She felt numb and yet felt an all too familiar sting that she had felt one time before. So she took the mug and drank it. The shock of the rum burnt her throat and she spit it out as quickly as she tried to chug it. As she continued to cough, Myers laughed.

"Here try this instead," said Myers. It looked the same but in a different mug.

"No thanks." Johanna gasped.

"Ah, it's only apple cider," he insisted. Johanna looked at him with disbelief. "I have to keep it hidden. There is no way I am drinking with my men. They would slit my throat in a heartbeat. I have to stay sober and alert at all times or I am dead."

"Well, that's an awful way to live, even if you deserve it," said Johanna as she drank the apple cider washing out the rum taste in her mouth.

"You mean sober and alert? I agree," he laughed.

"No, I mean always feeling like your life is in danger even with your closest friends," recently she knew about the always feeling like your life was in danger part.

"Ah you get used to it after awhile," Myers answered. He stared her down. "Listen, I know it's hard to believe, but they weren't supposed to kill the captain, someone put his gag on too tight."

"Is that supposed to make me feel better?" said Johanna. "What about the young deckhand? Why did you kill him too?"

"What young deckhand?" Myers asked confused. "Maybe he was a liability. I sometimes have no control over my men." He brushed it off.

"So, what are you going to do with me?" she asked.

"I don't know yet. We will be departing in a few hours. Maybe I will let you go before that," he started to leave the room, "or maybe I will sell you to the highest bidder. I know I could be paid a lifetime of wages for a lady like you."

Johanna heard the click of the lock on the door. She noticed the letter that fell to the floor. She knew it was from David. He knew all along that she loved him. She couldn't believe how betrayed she felt. What did she think, they were going to run off together and live happily ever after? Maybe if she lives through this, she will marry Malcolm or maybe Rene? What did it matter, she was in danger again and this time no one was going to save her. She stared at the letter that lay on the floor. Getting angrier every minute, she began to plot revenge until the candle went out leaving her in the dark of night. She could hear Myers speaking on the deck to someone.

"Thanks brother, I will take it from here," a voice laughed.

"Well, if you weren't family I would fight you for her. She is definitely beautiful,' said Myers. "You know we could get a pretty penny for her in the black market."

"I know, but I believe it is time for her to get to know me a little bit better. There is no one around to save her this time," the voice said.

"What about your comrades? Are you just going to desert them?" Captain Darren Myers asked his companion.

"Absolutely," he said.

"Is it that easy for you to make this choice?" Myers asked.

"Well brother, you know how the old saying goes, 'blood is thicker than water'," both men laughed.

Chapter 19

*A*s Johanna listened she couldn't quite place the other voice, but it seemed quite familiar. She was on the verge of presumption when she noticed a light from the floor below her feet. She hadn't seen before for it was overshadowed by the candle burning in the room. She leaned down and tried to peek through the cracks but the light extinguished abruptly and then she heard a voice from below.

"Are you going to open the trapdoor or do you want

Myers to have his way with you?" She felt the wood with her fingers and pulled the trap open. Hands grabbed her from below and brought her down with a quick hand over her mouth. The trap shut as soon as the door opened to the bridge.

Johanna was scared for she couldn't see who had just saved her since the voice was muffled by the trapdoor. She didn't know if she had put herself in a far worse predicament than she had just barely escaped from. If she knew anything about herself, she probably had.

They listened intently to Myers yelling out orders to find her while he paced the floor above them. Her rescuer's body leaned close to hers while they stood together at the top of the ladder.

He finally let go of his hold on her mouth and brought his fiery lips on hers in the darkness. She knew that kiss. It was hot and steamy and it was all she ever longed for.

"Are you okay?" the voice in the dark whispered softly in her ear.

"David," she whispered as her heart skipped a beat.

She felt relieved, excited and confused simultaneously.

David had never heard her say his name before. It made his body quiver and he quietly exhaled overwhelmed by the feeling. He kissed her again.

"Follow me," he whispered again as he took her hand and led her to a small opening in the wood. She loved his hand. It was warm and strong. She felt safe even if she was mad at him for stealing the map. She would save her anger for later.

"They were going to use this for cannons but decided they would rather use the ship for commerce. More money in it," David explained while they crawled through a small space.

To her surprise a boat awaited them with Jacob holding the oars. A makeshift ladder attached itself to the ship and they climbed down into the boat. The sun was about to peek over the horizon. Despite the situation, she was overjoyed to see Jacob. She gave him a big hug in silence. He in turn was just as excited and relieved to see her once again especially in one piece.

David used his strong arms to row and they

disappeared out of the ship's sight before they were noticed. Johanna still in shock from the whole experience sat quietly.

"Are you okay Miss Lee?" Jacob asked. "You seem a little out of sorts."

"I am just a little overwhelmed that is all." She tried to smile and not look at David. Her hand still feeling his in hers, although, he had already let go.

David stopped rowing and sat next her, he grabbed her cold hands that shivered in her lap. "They didn't hurt you, did they?" he asked with concern.

"I am fine, thank you, Lieutenant McPherson," she was grateful he seemed to care but her indignation toward him overshadowed that feeling. She felt betrayed by his letter in the locket and a bit foolish for letting him kiss her again.

David felt the coldness of her words. He let go of her hands and stood up to row once again. The tension on the boat was unnerving, and even Jacob kept silent until they reached shore.

"There is a coach waiting for us," Jacob looked down at Johanna.

"Where am I going now?" she looked at both of them. They both didn't know how to answer her. "Don't tell me you still need information from me that you have not already stolen from me," she looked at David with discernment.

Both men stared at her fury still not sure how to answer.

"We would like to discuss that with you," David said beginning to be annoyed by her unrelenting temper.

"I am sure you do," she said angrier with each passing minute. "I wish you would have left me on the ship at least I would know when I am being betrayed."

"Ungrateful little wretch!" David blasted her.

"Ungrateful? Am I to be thankful that you have me a prisoner once again?" Johanna didn't back down.

"I have saved your life!" he reminded her. "I could have left you there and you would have been taken to a black market auction. A slave to the highest bidder, is that what you wanted?" David scolded her.

"Okay you two. This isn't the time," Jacob interrupted their spat. "Let's get ourselves to safety and then you can have it out."

Reprimanded by Jacob, they turned their heads away from each other like small children both seething with anger.

In the early morning light they entered the coach still in silence until Jacob spoke. "Are you still heading for Virginia?"

"Yes, that is where people who love me are waiting," she said while she glared at David. He was still angry with her and stared her down with contempt in his face.

"We will let you go. We won't keep you prisoner any longer," said Jacob.

"Why would you do that?" Johanna confused.

"On one condition," David interrupted.

"Of course there would have to be a catch with you," she said toward David.

David ignored her jab, "you must tell us where to get the military plans that go with the map we stol…," he cleared his throat, "acquired."

"That," she smiled in triumph, "is because I never trusted anyone. It is in a dear friend's possession until I say otherwise."

"Who has it?" Jacob asked her.

"Safe, until my journey is complete," she smiled.

"What does that mean?" Jacob asked her.

"It means it is waiting for her in Arlington," David answered for her.

Johanna's smile widened with a smug nod at both men.

"Then I guess we are heading to Virginia," Jacob smiled at Johanna's cunningness.

Chapter 20

"I must make one stop before we go to the train station," Johanna insisted. David raised his eyebrows wondering if she could be trusted.

"Here? Miss him already?" David asked.

"I left something here. I will just be a minute," she hesitated than said, "He did ask me to marry him, maybe I am going to tell him yes," she announced proudly and got out of the carriage.

Jacob laughed at David's frown, "You have to love

her tenacity."

David looked up at Jacob with a half smile and then watched her disappear in the doorway.

"Johanna? You are still here in New Orleans?" Rene asked adjusting his shirt. Johanna noticed a woman exiting the room rather quickly.

Johanna had to laugh. "I see you weren't keeping a candle burning for me."

Rene smiled sheepishly and shrugged his shoulders. "I believe you have caught me," he didn't deny it. "If I told you it was to get over you, would you believe me?"

"Absolutely not, I have a feeling you were over me once you closed my carriage door." She laughed. He laughed too. "I have a favor to ask you."

"Anything," he smiled at her.

"The cigar box that I asked you to save for me, do you still have it?" she asked.

"Yes. It is in a safe place. Are you taking up smoking cigars now? You devil you," he smiled. "Do you want me to get it for you?"

"Yes please, I am kind of in a hurry." Johanna looked

back in the carriage's direction.

"I will be right back," Rene left the room.

Johanna felt like it had been a year ago that she was Rene's guest. Everything had changed. Instead of going to Virginia with Malcolm, (where he was she did not know), she was leaving with David.

"Here it is," Rene came back in the room and handed her the box. "Is the box what makes it valuable or what's inside?"

"Oh definitely what is inside," she smiled. "Oh, by the way, have you seen Malcolm?"

"I thought he was with you," Rene confused.

"No, we got separated. If you see him, could you tell him that I am catching the next train to Virginia? I feel like I should let him know," she said.

"He left you again?" he asked. "I told you he wasn't a nice guy. Yet you left me for him anyway."

"Rene, you know I didn't leave you for him, just for Arlington," she smiled.

"Are you traveling alone?" he asked.

"Oh no, I am not," she left it at that.

"Would you like me to walk you to the carriage?" he asked with a hint of sadness in his voice.

"No, I think it's best you stay here, for the last time you walked me out I could barely catch my breath," she smiled and he laughed his infectious laugh.

# # #

On the train David and Johanna sat in silence while Jacob slept next to them, head against the rocking window pane.

Johanna whispered to David, "darling note you left me in my locket."

David smiled. "At least I didn't steal your locket."

"No, I guess I have to be thankful for that," she frowned. "Why do you think you have stolen my heart?"

"I did, didn't I?" he smiled, not really looking for an answer.

Johanna ignored his insinuation, "And the telegram? How cryptic can you get, 'you're in danger, all will reveal itself in dew time,' silly don't you think?" she asked him.

"What telegram? I didn't send you a telegram." David insisted.

"Then who tried to warn me?" Johanna asked.

"I wonder," David seemed to know, but wasn't ready to tell Johanna quite yet. "How is it you seem to get yourself in to so much trouble all on your own?" David asked her. Johanna wondered the same thing herself.

"I am curious, why did Malcolm think it was quicker for you to take a merchant ship to Virginia instead of the train? It takes weeks longer." He asked trying to get her to wonder too.

"Oh. I might know," she said sheepishly. "He wanted me to marry him. I think he was planning on having the captain marry us on board."

"And you agreed to this?" he asked carefully.

"I said I would think about it," she answered softly.

"I see." He wasn't sure what to say. He felt a little betrayed by her.

"Where's Preston?" Johanna asked now realizing that he hadn't been around and quite relieved.

"I don't know. He hasn't reported in since yesterday when I asked him to do me a favor," David answered. "I fear we have lost him. He does love New Orleans."

"It is a magical place," she smiled thinking of all that she had encountered since being there.

# # #

"Well Miss Lee, we are at our destination," Jacob took her hand and they departed the carriage.

"I can't believe I have finally made it home," Johanna said smiling. "I bet my Aunt Mary will have the biggest feast tonight celebrating my arrival." She smiled thinking about her aunt's kindness and astounding hospitality to friends and strangers alike. "It will be so nice to see my cousins once again."

"Don't forget our agreement," David reminded her.

"You won't let me," she said.

They were awed by the Custiss-Lee House that sat on a grassy hill, pillars stood tall in front giving it a powerful majestic feel characterizing its owner. Johanna noticed something startling and familiar. No one was tending the gardens or milling around. It seemed to be strangely abandoned. Her heart sank when the door was opened by David who had come from the rear of the building. He saw the shock and disappointment in her face. All Johanna could see while she searched the first floor was white linen covering up furniture. The blur of white everywhere made her feel sick. She continued up the stairs alone. David tried to follow her but Jacob held his arm.

"Let her go," Jacob said.

Johanna ran through the bedrooms same white linen covered beds and tables. She entered one room realizing the bed had looked slept in. She stepped towards it confused and the door behind her closed. Johanna turned.

"Malcolm?" she was surprised to see him and suddenly felt afraid and wasn't sure why.

He smiled at her but it didn't look sweet anymore, it seemed more cunning and his eyes red and baggy, his face pale, as if he hadn't slept in days.

"I found you," he said in a whisper.

"What happen to you? Is everything all right?" she asked now noticing the revolver that he held in his grip.

"It is now. I have been riding for days riding ahead of your train. I only made necessary stops so I could save you," he whispered while he advanced toward her. He leaned in close to her and caressed her hair and then smelled it as if it were a sweet perfume. "Did you miss me?" he asked her.

"Yes," Johanna afraid of what Malcolm might do with the gun. "What happened to you?" she asked eyes still watching his trigger finger.

"When I met my contact he let me know what Myers was planning, but by the time I came back to save you, you had already escaped. I barely made it out alive," he now whispering in her ear. "I am so glad you are safe."

"Did you send the telegram to warn me of danger on the ship?" she asked him.

"What telegram?" he questioned her.

"Who could of it been from?" Johanna's mind raced trying to think of who would have known of her impending danger.

Johanna didn't know if she should try to run or run

away with him before Jacob and David came looking for her. He continued to caress her. His lips now came gently on her forehead and then her cheeks. It seemed to her he had taken with whiskey, but it wasn't on his breath. She stood still not making any sudden moves still watching his hand now noticing it shake as if he was shivering from cold. He tried to kiss her lips before she turned her head towards the door, not sure of what to make of the new situation she was in. Malcolm grabbed her chin with his free hand making her look at him.

"Malcolm, what are you doing, you're hurting me?" she questioned his roughness toward her.

"You have something that belongs to me and I need you to give it to me now," he stared her down.

"Well, that you will have to wait until we are married," she came out from his grip.

Malcolm laughed. "I need those military strategies and the map your uncle had you keep for him. I only have three days to return it. Your uncle needs it, its very important."

"I know Malcolm. You don't have to worry, I have it

here in the house, I brought it," she felt a little more reassured by his odd behavior. "Where is my uncle? Did he leave word to where I was to go, now that Aunt Mary has left," she asked worried about her future.

"You have the map too?' he asked her ignoring her questions.

"Well, I don't have it on me. Someone else does," she announced, "And by the way, we have guests downstairs."

Chapter 21

"She is taking too long," David looked at Jacob annoyed.

"She is very upset," Jacob said, "give her time."

"I think something is wrong," David said and then heard a muffled cry from above. David took off. He skipped stairs while his adrenaline flowed, thoughts raced of what was happening to her. He smashed through the door and Malcolm had his arm around Johanna and a revolver at her temple.

"Let her go Malcolm. This is between you and me," David insisted.

"Oh yes, this has been about you and me, you and her, her and me," Malcolm said as he swung the gun back and forth toward Johanna and then at David. "It's a bit of a lover's triangle wouldn't you agree?" he leaned into Johanna kissing her silken hair while keeping the gun pointed now at David.

Johanna mortified by the predicament she found herself in stood in shock.

"I see you have met my fiancée," he smiled at David. "I know you are familiar with what a fiancée is, right David?"

David stared him down waiting for an opportunity to distract him and grab the revolver out of his shaking hands afraid for Johanna's safety. She stared at David with fear in her eyes. It affected him more than he realized.

Jacob then entered the room startling everyone. David didn't hesitate and tackled Malcolm to the floor pushing Johanna away from him. The revolver tumbled out of Malcolm's hands. David's adrenaline skyrocketed as he grabbed Malcolm and kept punching him thinking about how he could have hurt Johanna. He didn't stop until he heard Johanna pleading for him to stop from behind.

Jacob ushered Johanna out the door when she began to cry for David to stop hurting Malcolm, taking the revolver that Malcolm had with him.

"Are you okay?" Jacob asked her as they descended the stairs and headed toward the drawing room.

"I am fine thank you, Mr. Evans," said Johanna still a little shook up by the unpleasant incident.

David grabbed Malcolm and headed for the first floor where Johanna was catching her breath. He looked at her with concern and then stared down Malcolm who was sitting on the floor with a gun now pointed toward him battered from the confrontation.

"Johanna, it seems your fiancée hasn't been quite honest with you," David said, "Malcolm why don't you tell her. Let her know what filth you really are," David accused Malcolm.

Malcolm wiping the blood from his lip, looked at Johanna and then to David, "I don't' know what your talking about."

"Let's see, you are actually a Union spy, not a loyal Southerner. You have been not only deceiving Johanna but also her uncle." David continued. "You knew all along about the papers she had in her possession which you failed several times to get from her."

"I will tell her no such thing," Malcolm still refused to admit his wrong doing.

"Yes, it is true. I am sorry to say he has deceived you Johanna. The pirate at the St. Charles Hotel, that was all him. He set it all up, paid handsomely for your capture. It backfired on him though; Rene saved you before he got the map. And at the steamship, he was supposed to come in like some hero and save you, but I got to you first. You were never really in danger," David explained to her.

Malcolm staring David down gritted his teeth, "I am not the only one who has betrayed you. McPherson here will do anything to get his hands on the map, including kissing Clarice on the balcony and making her believe he loved her while the whole time he has been betrothed to a girl from his hometown. Kathleen is it?" Malcolm asked.

"Aren't you getting married in a week?"

David stared him down, but did not deny it.

"Did he make you believe he loved you too, Johanna?" Malcolm smiled knowing the damage he was doing. "He is a master of deception."

Johanna swallowed hard. Jacob held her arm and squeezed it for support. She couldn't hide the disappointment in her face or the tears that welled up in her eyes. She didn't know which was worse of the betrayals.

"That is enough," Jacob said interrupting their confessions.

David watched tears slowly creep down Johanna's soft cheeks. It broke his heart to see her in pain in which he caused. He started toward her, "you have to let me explain."

Malcolm used this moment to his advantage and he grabbed the revolver from David's hand. He pointed it toward them still sweating and shaking.

"It appears I am now in control of this situation. Miss Johanna, give me Lee's papers and I will not kill your precious David."

"Don't listen to him. He is not giving it to your uncle. He is going to sell it to the highest bidder," David tried to persuade her.

"I don't care anymore," she pulled out the cigar box hidden in a pocket she made in her dress and handed it to Malcolm.

David and Jacob looked at each other realizing they were conned by her. It was in her possession the whole time. The sad part about it, David did have the cigar box, but thought they were just cigars and gave it back to her at the Beauregard House, trying to gain her trust.

"What is this?" Malcolm asked.

"The plans are hidden inside. Please just go," whispered Johanna sad that it had come to this.

Malcolm looked at her and then looked at David. "The map, I believe it is in your possession."

David stared him down not moving.

Malcolm pointed the gun at Johanna. "I said I want the map," he asked David once again.

"Don't hurt her," David pulled out the map. "It's here, just don't hurt her." He slowly gave Malcolm the map.

Malcolm watched how David looked at Johanna. He stared them both down, and then "Bam!" Malcolm shot Johanna.

"I believe now I have gotten what I came here for, my revenge on you," and he took off into the night.

"Should we let him go?" asked Jacob.

David didn't hear Jacob's questioned. He had already run to Johanna's side.

"She is bleeding, it's everywhere Jacob," cried David. He held her head in his lap. Tears had had already glossed his blue eyes, they slowly trickled down his unshaven face.

Jacob came to his side and leaned over Johanna inspecting the wound.

"It's okay David," Jacob assured him. "She's going to be okay."

"I can't lose her, Jacob," said David in shock. "I just can't."

"I know," said Jacob as he grabbed a white linen cloth that had covered a chair nearby and laid it over Johanna's now shivering body.

David thought he was going to be sick. The linen

looked more like a burial shroud. He prayed silently it would not turn into one.

Jacob put his hand on David's shoulder for support, "we need to get her a doctor."

David couldn't move. He was angry with himself for putting Johanna in danger and simultaneously filled with undeniable fear of losing her.

"I did this," said David. "I put her here. I as much as shot her myself."

"You can't blame yourself, David," said Jacob.

"I knew what Malcolm was capable of, I just didn't know he would go this far," David's voice cracked as he held back his tears.

"We will deal with Malcolm later, but now we need to get her some help," insisted Jacob.

"Okay," David wiped his tears. "Tell me what you want me to do?"

Jacob looked at his distraught friend. It broke his heart to see him in such turmoil.

"Why don't you stay with her," said Jacob realizing David wouldn't want to leave her side. "I will try to find a doctor."

David looked up at Jacob in desperation; tears filled his eyes once again, "please hurry."

"I will my friend," said Jacob. "You just keep her warm."

"David?" Johanna tried to whisper. Her eyes barely opened. Her face was paler than usual and her red lips seemed to be losing their color.

"I am here," he cradled her even more. "I am here."

Chapter 22

"Are you feeling better?" Emma Evans asked Johanna with a warm smile. "It's great to see you awake and out of danger."

"I am fine. Thanks to the both of you," she smiled up at Jacob and Emma.

"How's your shoulder?" asked Jacob.

"A little sore," she smiled. "I just can't believe I have no recollection of the past week."

"You don't remember anything?" asked Emma.

"Not really," said Johanna trying to recollect the last several days.

"You don't remember the doctor in Arlington or the train ride?" asked Jacob.

"Or David not leaving your side?" added Emma with a smile and a wink.

Johanna looked around the room, "where's is Mr. McPherson?"

"He had something he needed to take care of," Jacob said.

"Right," his betrayal came rushing back. "It's just as well. I don't really want to see him."

"He didn't leave your side for a week," Jacob defended David.

"Jacob, could you check on Daniel for me?" Emma cut in.

"Sure dear," Jacob was thankful for his wife, she would be able to get through to Johanna.

"I am so glad to finally meet you, I have heard so much about you," Emma smiled at Johanna.

Johanna smiled back, "Jacob and I have been praying

for you and Daniel's health. I am so happy to meet you finally too."

"You have caused quite a stir being here," Emma handed her a cup of tea.

"I am sorry, I never meant to be anyone's inconvenience," Johanna frowned.

"You are not at all. I just meant…" Emma tried to say.

"You mean being Lee's niece," Johanna finished her sentence.

"That, and well, coming back with David," Emma added.

"I didn't come here with him; it's complicated," Johanna didn't know what to say.

"He is supposed to be married tomorrow," said Emma. "Did you know this?"

Johanna's heart sank. It was true. "I knew he was to marry," she admitted.

"Does this bother you?" she asked.

"Not in the least," Johanna lied.

Emma eyed Johanna. "How about if I say I don't quite believe you? I think there is something between you and David," she said.

Johanna didn't deny it. She carefully watched Emma not knowing where she was going with this conversation.

"I think if you stay here, there won't be a wedding," she admitted.

"Then all the more reason I need to leave," Johanna said feeling devastated and still sore from the gunshot wound.

"You don't have to leave, you can stay as long as you like," Emma insisted.

"I am not a prisoner?" asked Johanna.

"Not in the least," Emma smiled.

"I appreciate your kindness, but," she looked at Emma desperately, "I need to leave."

Emma smiled warmly, "I understand." She hesitated and then said thoughtfully, "If I know anything, I know that God always has a plan. It will all work out, Miss Lee."

"Sometimes, I wonder after all I have been through, for who will it work out." Johanna's voice cracked while she held back tears that began to form.

Jacob interrupted with a slight clearing of his throat,

"I have a letter for you Miss Lee." He handed it to her.

"It's from my aunt," Johanna said surprised. "How did she know I was here?"

"She doesn't. It was left by a servant from the Custiss-Lee Mansion addressed to you. You were too out of it to give it to you earlier," Jacob answered while Johanna read the letter.

"There was a meeting my uncle attended at the Virginia secession convention. There were several decisions to make, she's fled to Ravensworth. She wants me to meet her there," Johanna said relieved she no longer had to bear being in David's hometown when he was getting married.

"Yes I know," Jacob said sadly.

"Will you stay a little longer?" Emma asked.

"Yes, you no longer have anything we need in your possession. You are not a prisoner but our guest," Jacob tried to say politely.

"Jacob," Emma whispered in an accusing tone.

Johanna smiled, "I know what you meant, but I cannot," Johanna's eyes began to tear and she held them on Emma.

Emma's concerned look on her face turned to a smile. "Miss Lee would you like to meet our son, Daniel?" she asked.

"Would I ever," she smiled.

# # #

"David, you brought Lee's niece here? If he knows this he will send troops to retrieve her," Mrs. McPherson warned her son.

"Mother, I thought she was dying. I didn't know what to do," David answered.

"You must have her return to her family. You can't put us all in danger," said Mrs. McPherson.

"I know, but there is a problem with that," said David.

"And what is that, pray tell?" she asked.

"I am in love with her," David confessed.

"David, you are to marry Kathleen tomorrow," she said in shock.

"I don't want to marry her. I can't marry her. I was never in love with her. You thought it would be a good fit and I just never disagreed," David now feeling sick about all the people he was hurting.

"I see. You have definitely put yourself in an awful predicament. How do you think this is going to work out between you and Miss Lee?" Mrs. McPherson now concerned for her son.

"I don't know, but I know if I don't find out I will always regret it," he said.

"Will you too regret that you broke an engagement to a lovely woman who has loved you since childhood?" she asked.

"My only regret would be if I married her under false pretenses. I don't love her," he insisted. "I never did."

"You will cause quite a scandal for this woman?" she asked.

"I would die for her," David confessed.

"That is extreme," she said.

"I know, I just can't live with out her," he admitted.

"Oh, it must be love then," she smiled.

David smiled back, "I know you will love her too."

"I am sure I will," she said. "Son, I encourage you to pray about this decision you are making."

"I do every day," he smiled at her.

"That's my boy," she smiled back at him. "If this is God's will then surely he will move heaven and earth for you and her to be together."

"So, you are okay with this?" he asked.

"I just want you to be happy, that is all a mother can ask for," she smiled.

"That I am," he answered.

"I can tell," she laughed. "You know what a scandal this is going to be among my friends?"

"Can you handle it?" he asked.

"Oh, I look forward to it!" she smiled.

"Thank you," he smiled and kissed her on the cheek.

"You have one difficult task ahead of you," she said.

"And what is that?" he asked still smiling.

"You must go and tell Kathleen," insisted Mrs. McPherson insisted.

David's smile disappeared. He sighed, "I know."

\# \# \#

"Are you sure you want to leave?" Emma questioned Johanna while they were alone. "I so much enjoyed your company."

"You are such a dear friend. I am so thankful to you," smiled Johanna.

"I am sorry David hasn't come around. I don't know what could keep him," she tried to make Johanna feel better.

"He has no reason to come here now. I have nothing he wants," Johanna frowned. "I have nothing to offer him."

"Oh, I don't believe that is true," Emma smiled. "Jacob told me how much David cares for you. He didn't have to tell me though I saw it for myself when he was at your bedside."

"That was probably led more by guilt than anything for putting me in this situation in the first place," Johanna frowned.

"It seemed more to me," Emma insisted.

"I think I am just causing too much controversy being here. I don't belong here, I really must leave," said Johanna.

Emma and Johanna were interrupted by a knock at the door. When Emma opened it a young lady stood with a basket of pastries and smile.

"Oh Rebekah, it is so nice to see you," Emma hugged her.

"Mother asked me to stop by and give you some pastries and welcome your new guest,' she said as she handed Emma the basket with a big smile toward Johanna.

"Thank you. This is Miss Johanna Lee," said Emma introducing them.

"It's nice to meet you," Johanna smiled back unsure of their new guest.

"Oh, it is so nice to finally meet you," Rebekah said enthusiastically surprising Johanna with a friendly hug.

Johanna was awed by Rebekah's excitement and hugged her back without any reservation.

"How is Daniel doing?" Rebekah asked.

"Oh, he is doing just fine, thank you for asking," said Emma with a smile.

"I must go," she smiled brightly again at Johanna. "I have so many things to prepare for you see."

"Thank you for the pastries," said Emma.

"Oh, you are very welcome. I look forward to meeting you again very soon," Rebekah said only looking at Johanna.

Johanna smiled, "as do I."

They watched Rebekah leave with a bit of a skip to her exit. Emma closed the door and looked at Johanna with a huge grin upon her face.

"Well, she was easy to befriend," Johanna said to Emma with a grin. "She was the sweetest girl I have ever met. I have never seen anyone overflow with that much joy. I wish I could keep her near at all times."

"Interesting you say that," said Emma.

"Why is that?" asked Johanna.

"Because Rebekah is David's sister," smiled Emma.

Chapter 23

"Oh David, you have finally come back," said Kathleen. She was surprised how happy it made her to see him standing there in front of her. He was as handsome as ever. She leaned in and felt him wrap his arms around her. His muscles tightened and she felt the strength in his arms as he hugged her. His hold lasted only a second before he let go.

Kathleen's mind raced through all the memories she had of him. All the lonely nights she waited for him, knowing one day he would come to her and they would be husband and wife. And now he was here, but it was different. She really didn't want to marry him. Now it was more the idea of him that she loved. She knew he really never loved her and doubted if he ever truly would. It was something she couldn't bare. She let go of her hold and decided to let him go.

"Kathleen," David didn't know where to begin or even if he should. He noticed the warmth in Kathleen's eyes harden, her manner changed in an instant, she held her head high.

"We are to marry tomorrow David," said Kathleen.

"I know we are," said David frowning. He tried to gauge her feelings. He didn't want to hurt her anymore than he had to.

"It hurts me to tell you this," Kathleen said.

She knows David thought. He tried to lean in to her and squeeze her hand in support, but she reeled.

"What is it Kathleen?" David asked.

She heard herself speak but she could not imagine where this courage had come from.

"You've been gone a long time, David. Sometimes feelings change, people change," she said.

David eyed her with confusion. He again tried to put his hand on her hers, but she put her own hand up to halt him.

"What are you saying?" he asked.

"I am calling off the wedding," she announced.

"I am sorry, I wanted you to hear it from me," David apologized thinking someone had told her about Johanna.

She interrupted him, "please let me finish," she paused. "I don't love you anymore David, and I am pretty sure you never loved me."

David was so taken back by her words. He was going to let her down. He was going to say these things, but not so abruptly and not so harshly.

"Are you upset with me?" David had no idea what was happening. This was not what he was expecting.

"No, David." Kathleen's harshness turned to its softness once again. As she spoke, she suddenly felt free. She hadn't realized that this was exactly how she felt. She saw the panic in his eyes but knew relief was in his heart.

She knew she was doing the right thing for both of them.

David still was feeling speechless. He wondered if he should try to change her mind. He suddenly felt afraid for his future. Life would be safe and normal with Kathleen. He was sure he could love her eventually, in time. Time was all he would have once he left the army. He remembered looking forward to coming home to family and friends, to familiarity. Everything had changed since then. Had Johanna been a siren in disguise? Was he making a mistake? David's muscles tensed, he could feel the heaviness of his decision.

This moment would impact the very people he held close in his life. "What should he do?" he wondered.

He had to make the right choice. The safe choice was Kathleen. But Johanna, he didn't think he would ever get her out of his mind or heart, even if he tried.

"I don't know what to say. I thought you would be angry with me, especially because I…" he didn't know how to finish, but she did it for him.

"You love someone else," she said.

"Yes. I do. How did you know?" he asked.

"I had my suspicions when I discovered you were here for a week and you never came to see me," she said.

"I am sorry," he apologized. "That was very insensitive of me."

"You thought she was dying. Why would you leave her side?" she asked with a knowing smile.

"You knew that too?" he asked sheepishly.

"David, everyone in town knew," she said.

"I am sorry," he apologized again. "I forget sometimes what a small town we live in."

"Is she feeling better?" she asked.

"She is, thank you," he said.

"Is she really Lee's niece?" she asked curious.

"Yes, I am afraid she is," he frowned.

# # #

Is the coach waiting for me?" Johanna asked Jacob while she tried to put on a brave face.

"It is. Are you sure you want to leave town without

seeing David first?" Jacob asked.

"Absolutely, I am sure he has a wedding to plan," Johanna said with a grim look on her face. She tried so hard to show her tough exterior even though her heart was broken within.

"He..."Jacob stopped what he was saying. He didn't know what to say. He didn't know where David was but he knew he would be devastated once he realized she had left.

Johanna hugged him and Emma goodbye and hopped into the carriage. The driver closed the door and through the window Jacob saw her do a small wave to him and then the carriage rolled out of sight.

"Where is David?" Jacob asked Emma.

Now that Johanna was out of sight on her way to Ravensworth, she let everything she had been holding in come to the surface and she sobbed uncontrollably. How could she let herself be so betrayed by everyone? She didn't even know where her journey had begun. How she had gotten so far off the beaten path. She always felt in control of her life. Even when her parents had fled, she knew it was the right thing for her to stay. It hurt sometimes, but sometimes decisions did. Her mind raced through the inventory of men that came in and out of her life like a swift breeze right before a storm's wrath. They all had promises of love and yet all betrayed her in one swift blow. It was disheartening to believe this pallid life she was leading could be hers. She was finally going to Virginia to be with family but now the excitement of it seemed more skewed and foreboding. She recited scripture that always gave her peace, "all things work together for good." She wanted to believe this but she could never be as an unhappy as she was right now. She tried desperately to not love David.

# # #

"Jacob, I am here to see Johanna. Is she awake?"

David asked with a smile. "I have great news to tell her, the wedding is off."

"David, it is too late," Jacob mortified by having to break the news to David.

"What do you mean it's too late? I am free to love her

now," David rushed to the room where he last saw Johanna. "Where is she?" said David scared now.

"She left, David," Jacob put his hand on David's shoulder to console him.

"Where did she go?" David asked.

"She left to Ravensworth to be with her family, where she belongs," Jacob answered him.

"What do I do?" David asked his friend for advice.

"I think you should let her go," Jacob said as he saw the surprise on David's face who wasn't expecting this from him.

"But, I love her," David said.

"All the reason more you should let her go. She is angry with you and she thinks you betrayed her. How do you think this is going to end? We have failed our mission because of this and trust me, Meade will make us pay. They will never let us leave the army."

"I will take the blame," said David still in shock of losing Johanna.

"We just got word that Virginia is considering seceding. It is only a matter of time Lee will give his resignation. Her family is now considered traitors," Jacob sadly said. "Everyone is going to be hurt by this, including you my dear friend."

David's mind was spinning. He had sprinted to Jacob's with such joy in his heart, happier than he had ever been. He was ready to confess his love to Johanna, and instead he found himself faced with the realization that his happiness was only fleeting. He left in a daze, his mind in a darkened fog. He pondered every possible situation and could not find a suitable solution. He had no idea where he was walking. His mind continued to race as his heart broke with each step he took. He suddenly found himself at his family's home standing at the doorway in tears.

"Son, are you okay," Mrs. McPherson asked noticing his somber demeanor and led him to a chair.

"She is gone," he whispered.

"Who is gone?" she asked.

"Johanna. I don't know what to do," tears slowly seeped down his unshaven face. "I can't lose her, but I don't know how to keep her."

"Yes you do! Listen to your heart," she smiled

wiping away his tears with her handkerchief.

"My heart has betrayed me," whispered David again, "It will never work out. We are now from two different sides. It is too late."

"You will fight for your country but why won't you fight for love?" Mrs. McPherson asked him.

David closed his eyes while he inhaled deeply. He then opened them this time with a new outlook and a new desire to take a leap of faith.

"Thank you," David kissed her cheek and disappeared out the door.

Chapter 24

"We are stopping for a short rest, the horses need water," said the driver as he helped Johanna out of the carriage.

"Of course," said Johanna.

"Hello Miss Johanna," Malcolm came up to her.

"Malcolm, what are you doing here?" Johanna scared of the man who shot her.

"I followed you. I wanted to apologize for everything. Can you ever forgive me?" said Malcolm with sadness to his voice.

"Malcolm, you shot me," Johanna confused by his apology.

"I know. I will never forgive myself. I had a terrible fever and I was sick for many days. I didn't know what I was doing. You have to believe me," he begged her.

"You tricked me, you betrayed me," Johanna continued. "How could you do this to me and my uncle?"

"That was a lie. I did not set you up with pirates and I did not switch sides. McPherson was confusing you," insisted Malcolm.

"Why did you come here?" she kept her guard still not trusting him.

"I am trying to tell you, I am giving up the life of a soldier if that is what you want. I am spending my days taking care of you until you can forgive me," he handed back her cigar box and map.

"You're given me these after all that? You are handing them over just to say you're sorry and then what? Say I forgive you right now, Malcolm, then what?" she asked. "Will you ask for these back? Did you realize you couldn't go to my uncle without me and the papers?"

"That is not why I am here," he insisted. "I thought you were going to stay with McPherson. When you left Harrisburg, I thought I might still have hope."

"You shot me, took everything in my possession, lied to me, and betrayed me like no other, and you think that I would just forgive you?" she asked. "Why is it that you and Lieutenant McPherson can betray me in the worst way and think that I will just get over it?"

"You found out I was telling the truth about him, didn't you?" Malcolm asked. Johanna refused to answer. "Let me take you to Ravensworth. Let me prove to you my deepest regret was losing you."

"Malcolm, I don't think that is necessary," she continued to search him with her eyes for any deceit.

"Please let me. I did try to keep a close eye on you after I recovered from my fever. I found out where you were and kept watch from a distance to make sure you were in good health and safe," he stepped closer not trying to alarm her.

"You mean to make sure the bullet you put in me

didn't kill me," Johanna stared him down.

"Johanna, I swear to you, I knew that David felt something for you. I had myself convinced that you loved him too. I was out of my mind with fever and jealousy. I thought if I hurt you, I would hurt him too. It was a terrible mistake. You don't love him do you?"

"No, I do not," Johanna said without hesitation as she bit her lip in anger.

"Will you forgive me?" Malcolm asked.

"I will try," Johanna said still not letting him get near.

"I will spend the rest of my days making this up to you," Malcolm stepped closer until he was face to face with her.

"I still don't know, I want to believe you, you don't know how badly I want to believe you, but the pirate, Captain Myers, on the merchant ship?" questioned Johanna.

"Think Johanna, what are David's companions last names?" Malcolm said at a whisper now.

"They are Jacob Evans and Preston...Myers!" Johanna shocked to find out that every time she turned around nothing seemed to be what she believed.

"And the truth shall set you free," whispered Malcolm as he slowly put his hand to her frosted cheek.

"I don't know what to believe anymore," whispered Johanna, just feeling as if she wanted to give up. She put her head in his shoulder as he hugged her tightly.

"I know it will take time, but I still have hope that someday you will consider to be my wife," Malcolm whispered.

It felt warm being in Malcolm's arms. When Malcolm mentioned marriage, it jolted her. She was reminded about David's marriage to Kathleen. She took a deep breath to ward off the pain.

"I knew you were ill Malcolm, I will give you that," Johanna relented. "Maybe we can discuss this later when I get to Ravensworth."

"Miss, are you ready to leave?" asked the driver.

Johanna nodded, "Yes, I am, thank you."

"This is wonderful news!" he gave her his best charming smile, dimples and all.

"I said we will discuss it later," she reiterated.

"Then I look forward to our next meeting," he kissed

her hand softly and then helped her into the carriage.

Malcolm stood in place as he watched the carriage ride out of sight. His smile had now morphed into a smirk.

# # #

"You have got to be kidding me," said David who had now come out of the shadows inside the carriage.

"What are you doing here?" she asked him as her heart skipped a beat confused by his appearance.

David ignored her question, "Well my Southern Beauty, I didn't think it possible, but you have definitely surprised me again. You would consider marrying him? After he shot you? Oh, you must be very desperate to get married."

"Desperation is what drove me to let you, a Northerner, kiss me several times," Johanna stared him down.

"Was it desperation or love?" David asked.

Johanna refused to answer. "Why would you bring

me to Harrisburg, to ridicule me in front of your family or to parade your little wife around in front of me?"

"Do you think that is why I brought you there?" David asked.

"It doesn't matter," Johanna frowned.

"It does matter to me," David put his hand on hers.

Johanna's heart pounded in her chest. His touch made her tremble. She looked into his eyes. His sapphire eyes she was convinced she would never see looking at her that way again, and here they were.

"Do you believe I love you?" she asked him.

"I do," he insisted.

"Well, you're mistaken," she said. "Not everyone is in love with you Mr. McPherson."

"No, not everyone, just you are," he insisted.

"How do you know that? How could you have possibly convinced yourself that is true? I have never giving you an inkling of hope that I would ever fall for a man like you. A Yankee for goodness sake," she continued with her insults. "You aren't any different than Malcolm, he betrayed me the same as you."

"If you think that I am anything like Mr. Graystone than you don't know me at all, Miss Lee," said David.

"Well, I don't care to," she lied. "It's all lies. No one seems to know how to tell me the truth anymore," Johanna turned her face toward the window to escape his spell he had on her. "My encounters with the pirates in New Orleans were not from Malcolm and you know it."

"I do now. I didn't then. I am sorry. I thought I knew Preston more than anyone but I too was deceived. I should have known he had pirate blood in him," David confessed with a bit of a chuckle. "He fits the profile doesn't he?"

Johanna smiled, "Yes, he definitely does."

"You don't know what restrain it took to not want to step out of the carriage and pulverize Malcolm," he said.

"Why didn't you?" she asked curious.

"Because I have made too many mistakes with you and I will never put you in harm's way again," he stared at her wondering what she was thinking. "So, where do we go from here?" David asked her.

"Well, you are getting married and I am going to live

with my family in Virginia, which is now planning on seceding," said Johanna "I guess this is where we say our goodbyes."

David sat next to her now, leaned in and whispered gently, "I am not getting married."

The words freed her from the pain that she had been carrying within her. She closed her eyes and took a deep breath to keep her from smiling. All she wanted to do was smile or giggle, or laugh, but there still was so many obstacles in the way. She felt his gaze upon her. She could hear their hearts beating and the horse's hooves clopping. David put his hands over her cheeks and brought her to him. He kissed her with so much passion she feared she wouldn't be able to stop. His embrace was all that she had longed for.

"What are we doing?" Johanna stared at David.

"It's called kissing," David smiled.

"You know what I mean. Where do you think this is going to go? We live happily ever after?" Johanna now faced with reality.

"Why can't we? You have to trust me my Beauty.

Have a little faith. It will all work out," David smiled and caressed her cheek.

Just then Johanna looked outside of the carriage and saw Ravensworth approaching and within its borders were soldiers surrounding its grounds.

"Those must be General McClellan's men," observed David. He knew he had to leave before he was noticed. "I have one favor to ask you," David looked at the map that Johanna was holding.

"You want the map," Johanna now feeling duped.

"It's not what you think," he said. "Jacob wants to retire and stay with his family in Harrisburg. Meade will never let him if we go back to him empty handed."

"So, it's for Jacob, not for you?" Johanna was still unsure of his intentions.

"Listen, keep the cigar box. I just need to bring the map back. Please I am asking you to trust me," he pleaded.

She bit her lip deciding her fate, "all right, I will give it to you, but it's not for you, I am doing it for Jacob and Emma."

"I know," he frowned and looked out the window.

They both felt the moment intensify. He would have to depart and leave her alone once again. To Johanna it seemed her once in a lifetime romance would come to an end once David stepped out of her carriage. A foreboding feeling crept over her.

"Wait," she whispered before he leapt out of the moving carriage. He seemed to know what she was feeling perhaps he was felt it too. He didn't say a word. He grabbed her with a powerful embrace, kissed her, and then jumped.

# # #

"Johanna, my dear, you made it," said Mary Custiss-Lee hugging Johanna. "I am so sorry for leaving Arlington before you came. Are you all right?"

"I am fine, Aunt Mary," smiled Johanna feeling the warmth of her aunt's hug. "I am happy to finally be here in one piece."

"You have been through quite a lot since your parents

left," said Mary with a frown.

"You don't know the half of it," said Johanna.

"Well, we can sit and have tea and you can tell me all about it," smiled Mary.

"That's sounds wonderful," said Johanna returning the smile.

"Your uncle should be here soon," said Mary. "He told me he appointed a young soldier to escort you here. Where is this young man?"

"It is a long story," sighed Johanna. "Maybe one I should write down one day, for I can't believe it myself, and I went through it."

"Was it that bad, my dear?" asked Mary worried about her niece.

"Yes, I would like to hear all about it," said a voice from the doorway.

"Robert, you are home," Mary ran to her husband, embracing him.

Robert smiled at his wife and then eyed his niece, "Johanna, I think you and I need to talk."

"Yes, I think we do," said Johanna.

# # #

Weeks had passed and although Johanna was thankful to finally be with her family, she missed David and thought of him often. No word came from him and she started to believe that maybe he really did only pretend his affections to get a hold of the map. Everyone was talking about the new Confederate States of America in which David was no part. Malcolm had continued to pursue her and she began to welcome the company. He did seem to feel regretful about shooting her and eventually she did forgive him.

"Johanna, do you truly forgive me for shooting you?" Malcolm asked as they walked the gardens.

"I do Malcolm," said Johanna.

"Will you say I do again to me in front of witnesses?" Malcolm smiled.

"Maybe I will," Johanna smiled back.

"You don't know how happy you have made me," Malcolm leaned in and kissed her cheek. "I must leave at once to New Orleans. I have been called to a meeting with your uncle at Fort Pike. I can't wait to tell him the news!"

"When will you be back?" Johanna asked.

"In two weeks, just enough time for you to plan our wedding," Malcolm smiled as he walked out the door.

"Wait, I can't plan a wedding in two weeks," Johanna tried to say but he had already left. "What am I doing?" Johanna questioned herself. "I must speak with Aunt Mary."

# # #

"Sir, I know I have asked you this before, but I am asking you again for leave for a few months," reminded David.

"I understand that, Lieutenant. I can't accept your request. I need you, you're my best soldier. If I let you leave now I am afraid you will never return, like your pal Myers," said General Meade.

"I told you, he never left New Orleans. I guess he

decided to stay with his outlaw brother and become a pirate himself,' admitted David. "It was a surprise to me sir. I had no idea he was related."

"At ease soldier, I know that,' Meade said.

"You have me on missions that anyone can do, I haven't even gotten to write a letter to my family in six weeks," David said now frustrated with his predicament.

"I know. We do thank you for your dedication and retrieving the map for us. Now that Virginia seceded and Lee followed like we predicted, it will be a detrimental asset. General Grant is looking for a few men to lead another mission. It's dangerous but I know that you can handle it, so I recommended you. Will you consider taking it?" Meade asked.

"What is it?" asked David.

"We need you to head to Baltimore and retrieve luggage that was taken by a mob from the Baltimore Riot. There was something in one bag that must be retrieved. Further instructions will be waiting for you at the train station where it was last seen."

"What in this bag?" David asked.

"A letter from Lincoln, let's just leave it at that," Meade said. "I need you to take this too."

David realized Meade had handed him the map that started it all. "I can't do that," he whispered.

"Yes you can. It's an easy task. Why don't you take Evans with you or if you prefer you can go it alone. Change your clothes, you're going undercover for this one," Meade ordered. "Oh by the way, Private Graystone decided to follow in Lee's footsteps and leave the Union, he was a traitor just as you suspected. He ended up marrying the General's daughter."

David sat in sheer disbelief. He whispered to himself, "You mean his niece." He felt like he had just been punched. "Sir," he said aloud, "I will accept the mission. But after that I am staying in Harrisburg to protect my family."

"I understand," answered Meade.

David rode hard into the night. Grief stricken at his loss he cried out into the abyss, "If you only had a little faith in me."

Chapter 25

*J*ohanna figured there was no way that David and she would ever be free to be together. March came and went with no word from Malcolm or David. Conflicts began to rise throughout the country. Ft. Sumter had fallen and in Baltimore a riot killed Union soldiers. It made Johanna sick to think it could have been David or Jacob. Virginia indeed had seceded and her uncle decided he couldn't fight against his own state and family. It was a hard decision for him to make.

"He has been out in the gardens for hours, just pacing," said Mary.

"What do you think he will do?" Johanna asked.

"I don't envy him, it seems no matter what he decides, he will be fighting against friends," Mary said sadly.

"Does it have to come to war?" asked Johanna fearful.

"I am afraid that is what it is leading to," said Mary.

The women continued to watch Robert in the gardens. Both of them filled with anxiety about his final decision for different reasons.

"Now, what about this Malcolm I have been hearing about?" Mary asked trying to distract them from the heaviness of the situation. "Do you want to marry him?"

Just then Robert entered the room. Both women looked up with concern.

"I have come to the final conclusion," he announced, "that I must resign from the U.S. Army." He stood erect confident in his decision. "I will accept the position as commander of the Northern Virginia Army."

Johanna and Mary began to cry.

"I cannot fight against my home state," he added.

To Johanna it was like a knife had just ripped apart any connection that David and she had together. She felt the heart strings break one by one leaving her with only one decision to make; how to get over David McPherson.

"Johanna," said Robert, "I am very grateful for your help in keeping my plans safe. I knew that I could trust you. I am sorry for putting you in harm's way getting it to me. Mary said that it caused a lot of heartache as well?"

"I am glad I could help," said Johanna. "I am just sorry the union soldier took the map. I found myself being deceived on several occasions. I didn't know who to trust."

"It is hard to know," explained Robert. "Sometimes you just have to go with your gut."

"Pardon?" asked Johanna not understanding his words.

"Go with what your heart tells you. It never seems to mislead," he said.

"My heart has made me love one who is now our sworn enemy," confessed Johanna.

"Johanna," Robert put his arm around her, "you are

free to love who you choose. I just want you to know that I have many dear friends in the North. I had to make a decision because of who I am. That is one decision you do not have to make. We will always be your family, always."

Tears welled up in Johanna's eyes. "Thank you for saying that, Uncle," she smiled. "It doesn't matter now. I fear I will never see him again."

"I am a bit confused. What ever happened to Malcolm?" he asked. "Are you not going to marry him?"

"I don't know, I haven't heard from him," she answered. "He told me he was going to meet you in New Orleans. Did you not see him there?"

"I never made it," said Robert.

"I am finding he is not very trustworthy," said Johanna.

"Nonsense," insisted Robert. "He is a fine man. I hand picked him myself to escort you out of South Carolina."

"Well, maybe he was delayed," said Johanna. She wondered if she should tell her uncle about him shooting her and then decided against it.

"I must leave. I will send word if I am in contact with Malcolm. In the meantime, would you continue to hold on to my cigar box?" he asked.

"Absolutely, you can count on me," she smiled.

"Good. I know it is safe in your hands. I will send for it when it is needed. Hopefully, this time it won't cause you as much grief," he said.

# # #

It had been almost two months since David jumped out of her carriage and out of Johanna's life. He had the map and didn't need her anymore she thought. She did have the plans kept safely in the cigar box skillfully wrapped around each aroma filled cigar. Her uncle had left it in her care once again until it was needed. She reread her Blackwood's Magazine, "it's a beautiful romance, but it is all so fleeting," she frowned and then closed the book.

"There is a letter for you Miss Lee," said one of the servants who handed her a sealed envelope.

"Now who could this be from?" asked Johanna.

Malcolm hadn't sent word, a reprieve for her she welcomed. She just wasn't sure if she really wanted to marry him. He had proven himself to be unpredictable and rather unreliable.

Johanna opened the envelope which bore her name. She felt the anticipation as if she were a child opening a special gift from a loved one. "Oh, it's from Abigail!" she smiled at first. As Johanna hurried through the short letter her demeanor changed. At first pleased to hear from her dear friend and then quite distraught by the news it brought;

Johanna,

I have scandalous news! You won't believe it when I tell you. I hope you are sitting down. Your dearest Malcolm Graystone married Clarice Beauregard yesterday. The wedding seemed to come up quickly but they say they were privately engaged for several months. I pray you are not too upset. You still have your number three.

Forever your friend,

Mrs. Abigail Jenkins

Johanna held the letter in her hand reading it repeatedly not quite sure what to make of it. She didn't know if she wanted to laugh or cry. She felt quite humiliated with a tinge of relief in her heart.

She went over to her night stand and realized the cigar box was missing. Malcolm had taken it before he had left and she, the fool that she was, didn't notice it until now.

Johanna ran to her aunt, who was in the drawing room sitting near the fireplace, a small shawl covered her shoulders.

"Aunt Mary," said Johanna in a serious tone. "I have news about Malcolm."

"Oh, is he coming back to marry you, my dear?" she asked.

"He is not, it seems he is already married," said Johanna.

"What do you mean?" Mary asked.

"He married Clarice Beauregard," said Johanna choking on her words.

Mary was stunned by the news and worried about

her niece's mental state.

"Oh, that is shocking news! That scoundrel, how could he do that to you?" Mary asked.

"You don't know Clarice," said Johanna frowning.

"He surprised us all. Robert really took to him," Mary shook her head. "He is going to be so disappointed."

"Yes, I am sure he is," said Johanna.

Mary put her hand on Johanna's shoulder to console her, "are you okay, my dear?"

"I actually am," Johanna smiled realizing she now felt liberated. "I should have known, but I was too wrapped up in my own affairs to see it."

"You know, Johanna, sometimes God closes doors so we don't walk through the wrong one," explained Mary.

"I think you are right," agreed Johanna. "Now what do I do with the door that still lies open?"

"That is a question only you can answer," said Mary smiling. "Is it a door you want to enter into?"

Johanna sighed, "More than anything."

"Than what are you going to do about it?" Mary asked.

"I am not sure yet," answered Johanna.

"Whatever decision you make, you know you have your uncle's and my support," assured Mary.

"I thank you. That means a lot to me," Johanna smiled at her aunt. "I don't know what I would do without you."

"You will never have to find out," Mary smiled back.

Johanna found herself at the gardens to ponder her predicament. She had felt better once she arrived. She understood why her uncle went there for prayer and meditation, it was a peaceful place. She sat in silence. Her mind raced through the last three months. She closed her eyes not sure if she should trust what her heart was telling her.

"What am I to do?" she asked herself. "What if he doesn't love me? What if this was all a ruse to get the map from me? What if I don't find out?" She continued to ask herself questions that needed answers.

Johanna smiled as she stood to leave. "I know what I must do," she put her hand over her heart, "I just need a little faith."

Chapter 26

"*S*ir, there is someone here for you," a train attendant tapped David on the shoulder and then pointed outside.

David, surprised by the intrusion, walked out to see who his visitor was. He didn't see anyone at first and then he thought his eyes were deceiving him. On a bench near by was Johanna with a distraught look upon her face. He thought he was mistaken or it was a dream, but he continued toward her anyway.

Johanna stood once he stepped closer to her. She still did not smile. She looked as if she had the weight of the world on her shoulders. He searched her face for a glimpse of the love she had felt for him that stormy night. He broke the awkward silence.

"You are well I see," he said.

She could barely speak, but said in a soft voice, almost a whisper, "yes." She continued to be on her guard.

"I have been away longer than anticipated and I could not send word," he said.

"Really, I hadn't noticed," said Johanna.

He smiled even with his heartache. She was being her stubborn self he loved so much. He wondered how he could have lost her.

"How did you find me?" he asked.

Johanna didn't answer him right away, she still felt unsure of her decision to find him, and a bit surprised by his attire.

"Are you working for the rail system now?" she asked a bit confused.

David laughed and adjusted his hat, "you know me, and how I love to be undercover."

"You like to pretend you are someone you are not," said Johanna not smiling.

"I never pretended with you," he said. "You married I heard, I guess congratulations is in order."

She looked confused at first and then kept her voice low and steady. If she didn't she would reveal her true feelings too easily and she wasn't about to let that happen.

"How does it feel to believe that I am married?" she asked him to test his feelings.

"It's......what do you mean believe? Are you not married to Malcolm?" he asked.

"No, I am not. He married Clarice," she said with a smile. "A fitting couple, they deserve each other, don't you think?"

"Oh, it was the general's daughter. I just assumed when they said it was Malcolm that he married you," David still processing this new information that Johanna was free to be his.

"Lieutenant, it's time to head out. I got the bag we

were looking for. It's urgent we leave right away, all hell broke lose at Harpers Ferry," a man interrupted who was also in civilian clothing like David. He ushered him to their horses.

"I am sorry. I must go," David touched her face.

Her heart beat faster. She could barely catch her breath. He was leaving. How could she stop him? He watched her struggle internally. She had a desperate look in her eyes. They both wondered the same thing. If this would be the last time they meet, the last time they look into each other's eyes. He didn't know how to tell her he loved her, there just wasn't enough time. It would make departing that much harder.

"I..." He didn't finish. Johanna ran into his arms and they kissed. A passionate goodbye kiss, the most desperate of kisses. He held her tightly.

She couldn't bear to let him go, but didn't know how to keep him. She couldn't say what was in her heart. It hurt too much to open that door. If she didn't speak the word, it would be easier to handle if this was their last goodbye. Johanna turned and ran and kept running, to where she had no idea. She couldn't stop the tears from flowing. She refused to look back. She couldn't figure out what led her to come here in the first place. He seemed more distraught by her presence. Her future suddenly felt empty. She had to process this new setback. "Where was she to go having a life without David?" she wondered.

He did not follow her. He hurt as much as she. He watched her slowly run out of his life. He closed his eyes, mounted his horse and rode off to his next mission. Her kiss still lingered on his lips.

# # #

"Miss Johanna, what are you doing in Baltimore?" asked Jacob surprised to see Johanna sitting on a bench looking out over the harbor. "It's not safe here anymore."

"I don't know," Johanna answered him as if she were in a daze, tears running down her face.

"Did you see David?" Jacob asked. "He is here."

"I did, please thank Emma for her letter," she wiped

her tears and took a deep breath. "She sent word to let me know you two were on your way here."

"You saw David? What did he say? Why are you here by the dock alone?" Jacob confused by her predicament.

"I was wrong, Mr. Evans. I came here like some harlot after a man who never really loved me. I guess I was chasing a dream," she felt in shock now.

"No, you were not. I am sure David loves you. I did everything in my power to prevent him from pursuing you, but it was no use, you were all he wanted," Jacob tried to console her.

"He must have had a change of heart," said Johanna. "Or he was fooling everyone to get the map from me. He has never told me he loved me, not ever. I came here to tell him I wanted to be with him but he just said goodbye," said Johanna.

"I don't know what he is thinking," said Jacob. "Unless of course, he thought it was in your best interest to let you go."

"It's in my best interest or his?" she asked.

"I don't know, both I suppose," answered Jacob.

"Look at all the heartache this has already caused."

"I think it's only heartache on my side. I convinced myself that he loved me. That he felt more for me then just wanting some military papers. I have been so wrong." Johanna stood up and took a deep breath. "I guess it would have never worked anyway, my uncle has chosen to fight against the Union."

"I did hear about your uncle. His decision has caused sorrow to many," said Jacob sadly. "I am heading to Harrisburg, why don't you come with me? Emma and I would love you to stay with us," he said.

"Thank you, but I just can't," she said in barely a whisper.

"I understand, but where will you go?" he asked.

"I am going home," she tried to smile.

"Virginia?" he asked.

"No, that is not my home anymore," she frowned. "I fear I do not belong anywhere."

"Emma will be in touch. She will be very upset with me if I don't make sure you are okay. Can I do anything for you?" Jacob asked equally worried about her. "Can I get you a carriage?"

"I will be just fine, Mr. Evans. I don't need a carriage to get to where I am going," she kissed him on the cheek. "Please know that what ever happens, it is for the best."

Jacob watched Johanna silently walk away as if she was in a daze. He had never seen her so beaten before. It broke his heart.

"You are not doing anything drastic are you?" Jacob asked worried about her safety.

Johanna didn't answer him. He wasn't sure if he should follow her or not.

Jacob grimaced, "What are you doing, David? You are going to lose her forever."

Chapter 27

"Here is one ticket to Southampton, England," the clerk handed Johanna a ticket. "Sailing alone?"

"Yes," she confirmed her worst fear, "I am alone,"

"You should be able to catch a train to Paris once you get there," he smiled.

"Yes, thank you," she tried to smile without tearing up again. She needed to be brave.

"I can understand why you would want to leave this

country," the clerk said, "you never know who is Union or Confederate, you can't trust anyone nowadays."

"No kidding," said Johanna as she held the ticket in her hand the weight of it seemed a lot heavier than it actually was. She walked toward the door. Her head felt as if it was in a dream, a very sad and lonely dream. Her heart continued to deaden with each beat. She stepped outside to get some air to clear her thoughts and there before her stood David.

Her astonishment kept her from speaking and she stood in silence staring at him. He did not change his expression for one whole minute to Johanna it felt like forever. His manner did not make her feel at ease.

David had no idea he sat in silence that long. His breath was caught in his throat along with his words.

"Are you going somewhere?" He asked her in almost a whisper stepping closer to her so they were face-to-face.

"I am," was all she could say.

"Yes, you are going to Harrisburg with me," he said with authority.

"I am not,' Johanna felt angry at him barking orders

at her. "Who do you think you are? I am not your Southern whore, Mr. McPherson."

"No," he smiled. "You are my Southern Beauty, and I…" he swallowed, "am madly and hopelessly in love with you, and I know, God willing it will all work out. You just have to have a little faith."

She stared at him. She wasn't expecting him to say this. She thought for a moment she must be dreaming or she must have finally gone mad. She didn't know what to say. Could this work out? She didn't know anymore. She had been waiting for the day that he finally expressed his love, but now that he did, she wondered how many people would be hurt by it. She eyed him with uncertainty. She didn't know even if she could believe him. Did he want something from her? She couldn't go through more heartache another betrayal.

"Did you hear me?" he grabbed her shoulders and held her up close to him, trying to make her understand. "I said that I love you," He felt desperate to get through to her.

"I don't know what you want me to say," she still felt afraid to let go. Could she trust him?

"Just say it. Why won't you finally admit it to me, to yourself?" he asked.

"Say what pray tell," she asked as if she didn't know what he was talking about, still guarding her heart.

"That you are in love me. That you can't live another day separated from me. That instead of logic, you followed your heart, you chose me," he said.

Johanna continued to hold her ground and stay guarded. Her mind raced. She couldn't open her mouth. She was frozen in fear.

"I see," David's eyes began to tear and he let go of the hold he had on her. "Then I guess there is nothing more to say," he tipped his hat toward her with a slight bow of his head and he walked away.

What had she done? What was she thinking? This is what she dreamed about, what she had been praying for. He was all she had ever wanted. She loved him with her whole being. How could she ever let him go or give him up? She stood there not knowing what to do. She watched him walk out of her life without even looking back at her, not even once. He couldn't do that to her. Not after all they had been through. She closed her eyes, took a deep breath, and opened her shielded heart in faith.

"How dare you walk away from me, Mr. McPherson!" she yelled angrier at him for giving up so easily in defeat. "How dare you walk away from the woman you love?"

He continued to walk on as if he wasn't listening, she bit her lip. "How dare you walk away from the woman who loves you?"

David turned and stared her down. He thought how beautiful she looked so vulnerable, yet hands on her hips as if she was in control scolding him. She had finally said it. She had finally stopped trying to convince herself that she didn't love him. She stood her ground unsure what he was going to do.

"Pardon, I didn't hear you," said David cupping his hand to his ear. "What did you say?"

Johanna's faced flushed and tears began to fill her emerald eyes but she said it anyway, "I said," she hesitated, "I love you."

"Well, then," David smiled relieved his tactic actually

worked on her stubborn self. He then ran to her and picked her up in his arms and kissed her like he never kissed her before.

Epilogue

"Who do you have there?" asked David as he came behind Johanna and slid his arms around her, "rocks?"

She smiled as she felt the warmth of his body and the coolness of a warm summer breeze on her face. "They were given to me by the Voodoo Queen in New Orleans."

"Ooh, sounds mysterious," said David.

Johanna began, "I didn't figure them out until now. One smooth, this represented Rene. He always knew what to say, charming, handsome..."

David interrupted, "Okay, okay, I got it."

Johanna laughed, "Did he really bother you that much?"

"Only when he was holding you in his arms," he smiled and hugged her tighter.

"Well, he did have an amazing kiss," she laughed.

"Hey, that's not funny," said David.

"Nothing will ever compare to our first kiss," she assured him. "The thunder and lightening just intensified it."

"And the fact that you couldn't stand me," he added.

"And Malcolm knocking you out," she laughed. "How can you beat that?"

"I am sure I can try," he insisted.

"I would love you to," she laughed.

"Were you ever taken in by Rene?" he asked seriously.

"Not ever," she said. "I knew he would never be faithful to me. He loved the fact that I wasn't taken in by his charm. That was why he found me so appealing. Anyway, he definitely was a lot of fun to be around. I am glad we could stay friends."

"Should I be concerned by his letters he writes to you?" David asked.

"You have nothing to fear, my love," she said.

"I think the only time I feared for your safety is when you were near Malcolm," said David.

"Was it my safety you feared or that I would fall in love with him?" asked Johanna.

"Both," he admitted.

She held out the other rock, "speaking of Malcolm, he represented this rock. One rough, no matter how hard he tried the wickedness in him continued to show."

"If your stubborn self would have listened to me in the first place, you could have saved yourself from a lot of heartache, or at least from being shot," said David.

"Then I wouldn't of known how much you really cared for me," she sighed.

"Yes, it seems I had to follow you across several states, pretend I was courting a ghastly woman, get into numerous fights with Malcolm, stay by your bedside for a week and then chase down your carriage for you to finally get it," he said. "It would have been simpler if you would have just believed me in the first place."

Johanna laughed. "Wait, you never told me you loved me until I followed you to Baltimore."

"You never asked," he said.

"How was I to believe that you loved me? Every time we were together you would insist on that bloody map and of course, kiss me. I thought you were trying to trick me into falling for you."

"I always told you the truth. I never lied to you," he said.

"No, you just didn't tell me about Kathleen," she said.

"Well, I didn't know how to tell you," he said.

"I am so glad she found someone. It made it so easy to befriend her since she is happy and in love," said Johanna.

"Yes, that worked out for all of us. It was quite awkward having to explain to her how much I loved you," he said.

It seems you told everyone but me," said Johanna.

"If you wouldn't have left Harrisburg in such a hurry,

I would have told you myself," he said.

"You could have told me when you hijacked my carriage," she said.

"I just thought you knew," he answered.

"No, you just insisted that I loved you," she said.

"I wasn't wrong," said David.

"No, you were not," she smiled.

"And that one?" he pointed to the last rock she held.

"This one, oh, it seems rough on the outside, but," she opened up the rock to show its beauty, 'a treasure to behold.' This represented you," she smiled.

"You didn't realize until now that I am a treasure?" he mocked.

"Oh, I knew you were something," she smiled. They both laughed. "Want to help me do the honors?" She handed him one.

"Of course," They each took a rock and skipped it into the pond. At the end of the pond's shore, a dragonfly whizzed by inhaling the sweet scent of swamp lilies. "Let's keep this one just in case you forget how valuable I am." He held up the small geode. She laughed.

"Have you heard from your uncle?" asked David.

"Not recently. I know he is safe. Aunt Mary writes and keeps me informed without divulging any information of his whereabouts," said Johanna.

"I am sorry this conflict has been so hard on you," said David seriously.

"I just want it to be over. It saddens me that there are those who are fighting against friends and family," she said.

"I know. We will make it through this," said David trying to assure her. "I will keep you safe here in Harrisburg, no matter the cost."

"I do love you, Mr. McPherson," said Johanna smiling again. She then turned to him and searched his handsome face, "are you happy?"

He kissed her softly and then whispered in her ear, "Ever since I captured my Southern Beauty."

Author's Note

Southern Beauty is based on a loose interpretation of history. I spent many years researching the end of the antebellum era and the beginning of the civil war.

Robert E. Lee did have family that fled to Paris, France, because of financial ruin, although they did not have a daughter named Johanna.

Mary Custiss-Lee left Arlington and fled to Ravensworth but it wasn't until after her husband accepted the commission as a major general of the Confederate Army. For the story I needed her to have left much earlier. General Lee did not have a place in South Carolina, and there is no record of him ever visiting the South before his resignation.

General P.G.T. Beauregard was stationed at Ft. Sumter and did have a son, Rene. Rene was about 19 when the Civil War broke out. He did not have a twin sister.

The Beauregard family was from New Orleans where at the time lived the famous Voodoo Queen, Marie Laveau, and her daughter. Marie was a hairdresser to the elite. It is believed by listening to her patron's gossip and instilling fear in their servants is how she became so powerful. You have to think, if she knew everyone in town, then I am sure she did know the Beauregard family.

As for the cigar box, there was actually Lee's battle plans found wrapped around cigars by a private in the Union before the battle of Antietam at an abandoned Confederate campsite.

If you are still curious about other historical facts in Southern Beauty, I suggest the following;

Nationalcivilwarmuseum.org

Civilwar-online.com (Mary Jeffreys Bethel diary)

Confederatemuseum.com

Bkhouse.org (Beauregard-Keyes House)

Civiwarwomenblog.com

Nps.gov/fosu/index.htm

Made in the USA
Charleston, SC
20 March 2013